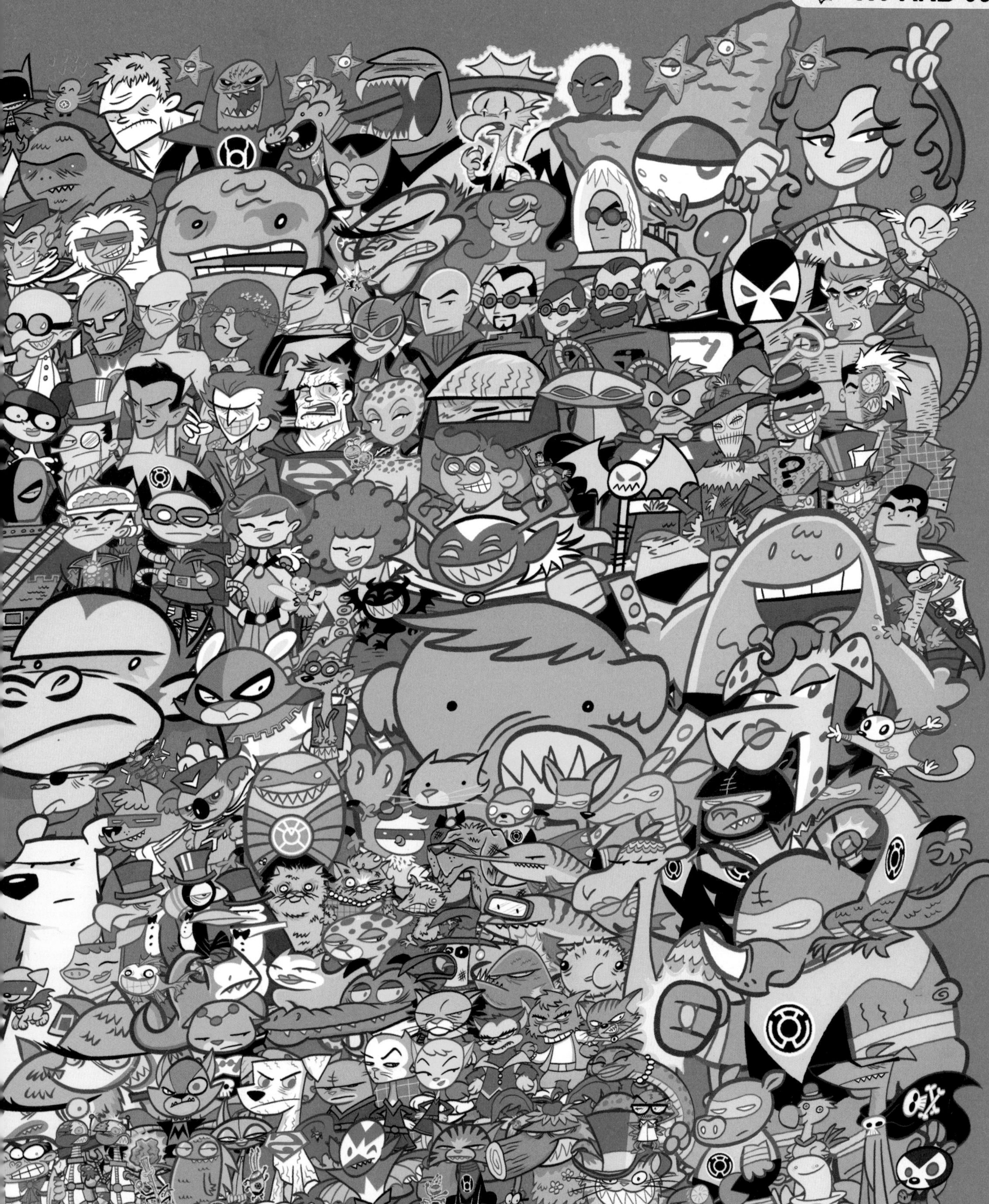

DC SUPER-PETS!™

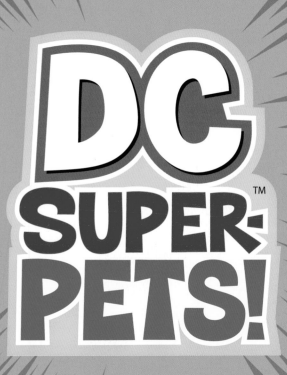

by Steve Korté

CHARACTER ENCYCLOPEDIA!

illustrated by
Art Baltazar

foreword by
Geoff Johns

Picture Window Books™
a capstone imprint

TABLE OF CONTENTS!

82　84　85　85　86　　　87　　　88　89　89　90

90　91　　　92　　　93　93　　　94　　　94　95　95

96　96　97　97　98　98　99　99　100　101　101　102

102　　　　103　　　　104　105　　105　　　106

　　106-107　　　　　　108　　　　109　109　110　111　111

112　112　　　113　　　114　115　　　　116

117　118　119　119　　　　120-121

KEY!

DC Super-Pets come in many shapes, sizes, and types. Use these handy symbols to identify each creature's classification:

- MAMMAL
- AMPHIBIAN
- ARACHNID
- WORM
- ROBOT
- BIRD
- FISH
- CRUSTACEAN
- HUMANOID
- OTHER
  - Magic beings
  - Imps
  - Demons
  - Inanimate objects
- REPTILE
- INSECT
- MOLLUSK
- ALIEN

FOREWORD!

Behind every smiling DC Super Hero and every cackling DC Super-Villain is...a DC Super-Pet! Or at least there is now, thanks to the creative people behind the wonderful book you hold in your hands!

So...what is a Super-Pet and where did they come from? Let me tell you.

Just like all super heroes started with the original and best super hero of them all—Superman—all superpowered pets started with Superman's Dog—Krypto! Before Jor-El and Lara sent baby Kal-El into space they put their family pet Krypto in a rocket of his own and launched it away from Krypton! Krypto's rocket was sent off course and lost in space. It wasn't until years later that the rocket finally found its way to Earth and back to the boy now known as Clark Kent. Under Earth's yellow sun, Krypto gained all of the fantastic and wonderful powers Clark did—and for a dog even more! Krypto became a hero in his own right, saving Smallville from natural disasters, chasing meteorites through space, and stopping the bad guys (and dogs).

After Krypto appeared, so did Superman's cousin, Supergirl! She had pets of her own, including Streaky the Super-Cat. The Superman Super-Pet Family grew with Beppo the Super-Monkey and Comet the Super-Horse.

Soon more and more super heroes found both pets and animal pals that helped them save the day. Super-Pets started to appear everywhere! Batman had his canine sleuth Ace the Bat-Hound help him solve crimes! Aquaman protected the Seven Seas with Tusky and Topo while Salty the Aquadog watched over the shores! Shazam! got help with his math homework from his talking tiger friend Tawky Tawny! And the Green Lanterns had animals join their Corps like the alien squirrel B'dg, who battled against the mischievous Orange Lantern gloop monster Glomulus and the grumpy Red Lantern cat Dex-Starr!

Within the DC Comics Universe you will find Super-Pets of all kinds—from dogs to cats to horses to seahorses! They are as lovable and loyal as our own animal pets and pals. This book is a celebration of our friendship with the animal world—be a hero yourself and show the animals in your life how much you love them!

The world would be a much lesser place if it weren't for the Super-Pets in our lives!

Geoff Johns
Chief Creative Officer, DC Entertainment

Dedicated to my bulldog, Buddy, who has the amazing power to eat food at lightning speeds.

HERO PETS!

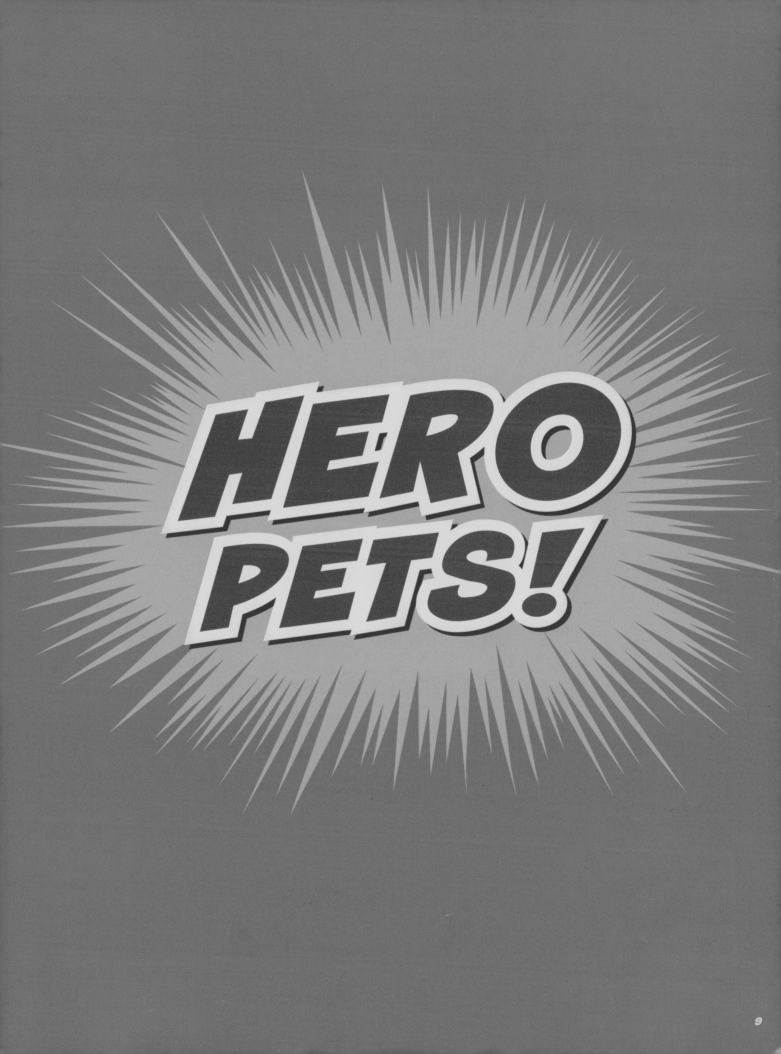

KRYPTO

Super-hearing

X-ray Vision

FLIGHT
Krypto can soar through the sky at super-speed.

Super-smell

S-shield

Strong Tail

Super-speed

HEAT VISION
Krypto can blast ultra-hot beams from his eyes to vaporize water or melt most materials on Earth.

FREEZE BREATH
The Super-Dog is able to blow super-cold air from his lungs, freezing anything instantly.

STATS

SPECIES: Super-Dog
BIRTHPLACE: Krypton
FOOD: Ka-pow! chow

SECRET BIO:
As a young pup, Krypto grew up on the planet Krypton, Superman's home world. Just weeks before Krypton exploded, the Super-Dog escaped aboard an experimental rocket ship. On Earth, the sun gave Krypto the same superpowers as his master, the Man of Steel.

WEAKNESSES:
Kryptonite
Magic

AFFILIATION:
Legion of Super-Pets
Space Canine Patrol Agents

SUPER HERO OWNER
SUPERMAN

ALLIES: **FOES:**

PUREBRED HERO!

Krypto the Super-Dog comes from a long line of Super-Pets—all picks of their litters!

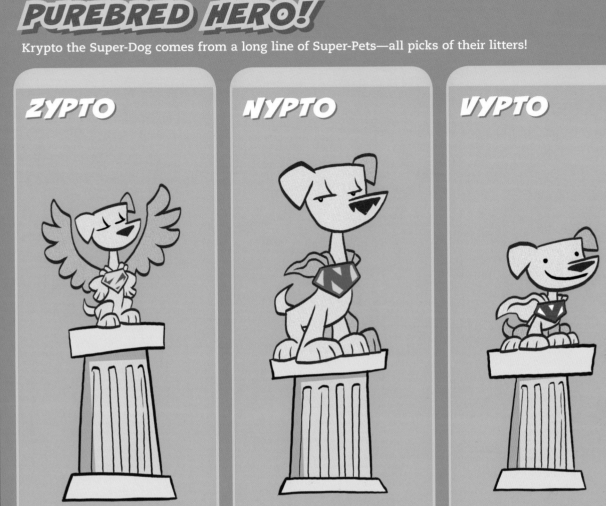

ZYPTO

A strange serum gave Krypto's father, Zypto, wings to fly through the air!

NYPTO

An alien's ray made Krypto's grandfather, Nypto, the largest dog ever known!

VYPTO

Krypto's great-grandfather, Vypto, didn't have any superpowers, but he was the smartest dog of all!

FURRY FACTS!

DOGHOUSE OF SOLITUDE
Like Superman, Krypto has his own getaway spot. He built the Doghouse of Solitude out of floating meteor fragments.

SECRET IDENTITY
On Earth, Superman is known as Clark Kent. Krypto has his own secret identity—an average dog named Skip (*see page* 16).

LEADER OF THE PACK
Krypto is the leader of the Space Canine Patrol Agents (*see page* 12). These powerful pooches protect the universe from evil.

SPACE CANINE PATROL AGENTS

KRYPTO (LEADER)
BREED: Super-Dog
POWERS: Flight; heat vision; X-ray vision; super-speed; super-strength; super-breath
FOOD: Ka-pow! chow

CHAMELEON COLLIE
BREED: Collie
POWER: Shape-shifting
FOOD: Space chow

TAIL TERRIER
BREED: Scottish terrier
POWER: Elastic tail
FOOD: Gummy bones

FURRY FACT!

LEADER NO MORE!
After failing the S.C.P.A., Krypto was stripped of his cape. To win back the team's trust (and get out of their doghouse), Krypto proved he was still the pride of the pack.

HOT DOG
BREED: Dachshund
POWER: Fire
FOOD: Corn dogs

PAW POOCH
BREED: Dalmatian
POWER: Multiple paws
FOOD: Tacos

ALLIES: **FOES:**

TUSKY HUSKY

BREED: Siberian husky
POWER: Giant tusk
FOOD: Corn on the cob

MAMMOTH MUTT

BREED: Mini poodle
POWER: Super-growth
FOOD: Cotton candy

BULL DOG

BREED: English bulldog
POWER: Sharp horns
FOOD: Bologna

PROPHETIC PUP

BREED: Jack Russell terrier
POWER: Crystal ball cranium
FOOD: Rock candy

STATS

BIO:
A powerful pack of pooches, the Space Canine Patrol Agents (S.C.P.A.) obey the message of their sacred oath:
"Big dog! Big dog! Bow wow wow! We'll crush evil! Now, now, now!"

S.C.P.A. HEADQUARTERS
The location of the Space Canine Patrol Agency is top-secret. S.C.P.A. members hold meetings at the Doghouse, as well as plan their defense against their feline foes, the Cat Crime Club (*see page* 113).

BIG DOG SIGNAL
When the "Big Dog" constellation (the official emblem of the S.C.P.A.) shines in the sky, Krypto is always ready to offer a hand—er, paw—to his fellow pets.

BEPPO

SUPER-STRENGTH
For a miniature-sized monkey, Beppo has gorilla-sized strength!

Super-smell

Heat & X-ray Vision

Super-hearing

Strong Tail

Super-speed

Super-breath

S-shield

FLIGHT
Beppo is a high-flyin' chimp!

MONKEY BUSINESS
The Super-Monkey isn't afraid to have a little fun!

What do you get when two monkeys fight over a banana?

A banana split!

SECRET BIO:
On the planet Krypton, Beppo belonged to Superman's father, Jor-El. Moments before the planet exploded, baby Superman escaped aboard a tiny rocketship. He wasn't alone! Beppo hitched a ride as well. On Earth, the Super-Monkey has the same superpowers as the Man of Steel, fueled by his adopted planet's yellow sun.

WEAKNESSES:
Kryptonite
Magic

SUPER HERO OWNER

SUPERMAN

ALLIES: **FOES:**

SUPER-TURTLE

SUPER-STRENGTH
Super-Turtle's shell is shockingly strong!

Heat & X-ray Vision

FREEZE BREATH
Super-Turtle can blast super-cold air from his lungs, making this cold-blooded animal even cooler.

Super-smell

Super-speed

Flight

HELPING HAMMER
The mythical hero Steel Turtle is a very powerful friend of Super-Turtle.

FEELING GREEN
The radioactive material known as Kryptonite is one of Super-Turtle's greatest weaknesses. These pieces of the destroyed planet Krypton can slow even the most heroic turtle on Earth.

STATS

SPECIES: Super-Turtle
BIRTHPLACE: Galapagon
FOOD: Turtle treats

SECRET BIO:
Born on an all-turtle island on Krypton, Tur-Tel made a slow—but steady—escape from his doomed home planet. On Earth, he gained the same superpowers as the Man of Steel and became Super-Turtle, the Turtle of Steel.

WEAKNESSES:
Kryptonite
Magic

FUN FACT!
Super-Turtle's father on his home planet was named Shh-Ell!

SUPER HERO OWNER
SUPERMAN

ALLIES: **FOES:**

THE DAILY PLANET PET CLUB

SKIP (KRYPTO)

BREED: Unknown
POWER: Disguising
FOOD: Ice cream

When hounding around the city of Metropolis, this Super-Dog hides his secret identity. Krypto sheds his red cape and applies a brown patch on his back. He becomes Skip, the regular ol' mutt of reporter Clark Kent.

OWNER

CLARK KENT (SUPERMAN)

At the Daily Planet Building, Superman ditches the blue and red uniform for a suit, tie, and glasses. As mild-mannered reporter Clark Kent, he always gets the scoop.

SCOOP

BREED: Chihuahua
POWER: Scooping
FOOD: Ice cream

OWNER

LOIS LANE

Reporter at the *Daily Planet* newspaper and friend of Clark Kent.

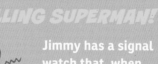

FUN FACT!

CALLING SUPERMAN!

Jimmy has a signal watch that, when pushed, calls for Superman's help!

ALLIES: **FOES:**

BIO:

To protect themselves, and their families and friends, super heroes and Super-Pets must keep their identities a secret. On Earth, Superman is known as Clark Kent, a reporter. He works at a newspaper called the *Daily Planet* with Lois Lane, Jimmy Olsen, and Perry White, who all have their own four-legged friends!

THE DAILY PLANET BUILDING!

The Daily Planet Building— and its giant, golden rooftop globe—is an iconic part of the Metropolis city skyline.

FRECKLES

BREED: Dalmatian
POWER: Spotting crimes
FOOD: Hot peppers

GUTENBERG

BREED: German shepherd
POWER: Sniffing out stories
FOOD: Squid ink pasta

OWNER
JIMMY OLSEN

Cub reporter and photographer for the *Daily Planet* newspaper.

OWNER
PERRY WHITE

Editor-in-chief at the *Daily Planet* newspaper.

FUZZY

SPECIES: Krypto Mouse
BIRTHPLACE: Smallville, Kansas
FOOD: Blue cheese

SECRET BIO:
The pet of Smallville resident Tommy Ewell, Fuzzy the Krypto Mouse gained his superpowers after being exposed to green Kryptonite in the laboratory of a local scientist named Professor Egglehead. He gained all the same superpowers as Superboy and became the Boy of Steel's newfound pal.

WEAKNESSES:
Kryptonite
Magic

SUPER-HEARING
With mighty ears, this Super-Pet can hear a mouse squeak a mile away!

Heat & X-ray Vision

Super-smell

Super-breath

Flight

S-shield

Strong Tail

Super-speed

SUPER-STRENGTH
Despite his super-small size, this mini mouse packs a powerful punch!

THE FORTRESS OF SOLITUDE
Even a superpowered mouse needs to relax sometimes. On Earth, the Fortress of Solitude is Superman's secret hideout. His pets and pals have access to this safe zone of valuable weapons, high-tech gadgets, and Kryptonian artifacts.

SUPER HERO OWNER

SUPERBOY

ALLIES: **FOES:**

SUPER-SQUIRREL

SUPER-TEETH
With this ultra-hard teeth, Super-Squirrel can crack macadamia nuts or crack a case!

Super-hearing

Heat & X-ray Vision

Super-smell

Super-breath

S-shield

Super-strength

Strong Tail

FLIGHT
You'd be nuts to call this Super-Squirrel a glider. He soars to the highest heights!

Super-speed

GET THE LEAD OUT!
Like all Kryptonians, Super-Squirrel cannot see through objects made of lead, like this pipe. However, lead isn't always so bad. This earthly substance can also block the harmful effects of Kryptonite (*see page* 22).

STATS

SPECIES: Super-Squirrel
BIRTHPLACE: Krypton
FOOD: Macadamia nuts

SECRET BIO:
Born on Superman's home planet of Krypton, Super-Squirrel became a powerful member of the Just'a Lotta Animals, an animal super hero team, which includes Batmouse, Wonder Wabbit, Green Lambkin, and many others. Super-Squirrel has the same powers as his owner, Superboy.

WEAKNESSES:
Kryptonite
Magic

SUPER HERO OWNER
SUPERBOY

ALLIES: **FOES:**

COMET

SPECIES: Super-Horse
BIRTHPLACE: Greece
FOOD: Oatmeal cookies

SECRET BIO:
An ancient Greek spell gave Comet the same powers as Supergirl and her Kryptonian family. The Super-Horse also gained the power of telepathy, or the ability to read minds.

WEAKNESSES:
Magic

FUN FACT!
Because Comet wasn't born on the planet Krypton, the Super-Horse is not affected by green Kryptonite (see page 22).

Super-hearing

MIND READING
Comet's powers allow him to read the minds and thoughts of others.

Heat & X-ray Vision

Flight

S-shield

Super-smell

Super-breath

Strong Tail

SUPER-STRENGTH
Comet's powerful hind legs catapult him into the skies with one leap!

SUPER-SPEED
This Super-Horse is always ready to giddyup and go!

What did the pony say when it fell down?

"I've fallen, and I can't giddyup!"

SUPER HERO OWNER
SUPERGIRL

ALLIES: **FOES:**

STREAKY

HEAT VISION
Even a steel kitty crate couldn't hold this Super-Cat. His heat vision melts metal!

SUPER EARS
Like his friend Fuzzy, this Super-Pet can hear a cat burglar at work from miles away!

X-ray Vision

Super-strong Tail

Super-smell

S-shield

Super-speed

Lightning Bolt

Flight

FREEZE BREATH
When the situation heats up, Streaky keeps things cool with his freeze breath.

What do cats eat for breakfast?
Mice Crispies!

SPECIES: Super-Cat
BIRTHPLACE: Earth
FOOD: Milk and sushi

SECRET BIO:
While performing an experiment with X-Kryptonite, Supergirl turned her pet cat into a Super-Cat! Streaky has the same powers as the Girl of Steel.

WEAKNESSES:
Magic

FUN FACT!
Born on Earth, Streaky is not affected by green Kryptonite. However, red Kryptonite (*see page 22*) makes this Super-Cat sleepy.

SUPER HERO OWNER
SUPERGIRL

ALLIES: **FOES:**

WHIZZY

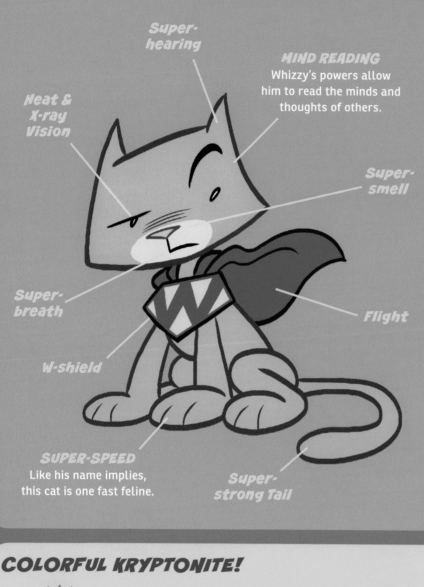

Super-hearing

MIND READING
Whizzy's powers allow him to read the minds and thoughts of others.

Heat & X-ray Vision

Super-smell

Super-breath

W-shield

Flight

SUPER-SPEED
Like his name implies, this cat is one fast feline.

Super-strong Tail

STATS

SPECIES: Super-Cat
BIRTHPLACE: Earth
FOOD:
Vanilla milkshakes

SECRET BIO:
Whizzy the Super-Cat is Streaky's (*see page 21*) family member from the 30th century. This futuristic feline has the same superpowers as his pal, Supergirl, the Girl of Steel. He also has the power to read minds, called telepathy. Unlike Kryptonian super heroes, Whizzy is not affected by the draining powers of green Kryptonite.

WEAKNESS:
Magic

SUPER HERO PAL

SUPERGIRL

COLORFUL KRYPTONITE!

GREEN KRYPTONITE
Drains the powers of heroes from Krypton.

RED KRYPTONITE
Varying effects that last only 24 hours.

X-KRYPTONITE
Created by Supergirl to combat green Kryptonite.

BLUE KRYPTONITE
Enhances Kryptonian powers, but harmful to Bizarro.

ALLIES: **FOES:**

SPACE CAT PATROL AGENTS

ATOMIC TOM

BREED: Space Cat
POWER: Nuclear *fursion*
FOOD: Tuna meltdowns

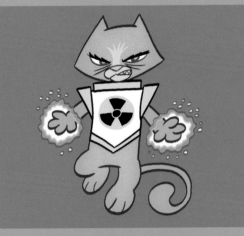

CRAB TABBY

BREED: Space Cat
POWER: Cracking cases
FOOD: Crab salad

POWER PUSS

BREED: Space Cat
POWER: Static electricity
FOOD: Energy drinks

SECRET BIO:
The Space Cat Patrol Agency is the feline branch of the Space Canine Patrol Agency (*see page 12*). These crime-fighting kitties help defend the universe against evildoers of all breeds. Like their canine couterparts, the Space Cats obey the message of their sacred oath: *"Big cat! Big cat! Meow meow meow! We'll crush evil! Now, now, now!"*

SUPER HERO PAL

ELASTIC LAD

ALLIES: **FOES:**

ACE

Ultra-hearing

BAT COWL
The high-tech mask protects Ace's secret identity.

ULTRA-SMELL
The Bat-Hound's powerful nose sniffs out trouble. He's known as the World's Greatest Dog-tective.

Utility Collar

Bat-Symbol

Fireproof Cape

Powerful Paws

Springy Hind Legs

LOYAL FRIEND
Batman has many enemies but one very loyal friend: Ace! When the Bat-Hound's not fighting crime, he keeps his billionaire master, Bruce Wayne, company at Wayne Manor.

What kind of dog has the most ticks?

A watch dog!

STATS

SPECIES: German shepherd

BIRTHPLACE: Gotham City

FOOD: Crime fighter crunchies

SECRET BIO:
Batman found Ace while solving a case in Gotham City. Unable to locate Ace's owner, the Dark Knight kept the dog and nicknamed him "The Bat-Hound." Ace considers himself Batman's partner, not his pet. The Bat-Hound uses high-tech gadgets, tools, and weapons to help Batman solve crimes in Gotham City.

SUPER HERO PARTNER

BATMAN

ALLIES: **FOES:**

HIGH-TECH HERO!

Like his super hero partner, Batman, Ace has many high-tech weapons and gadgets to fight crime in Gotham City. Check out a few of the Bat-Hound's favorite toys!

Batarang!

Utility Collar!

Rebreather!

Grapnel Gun!

Batrope!

Gas Mask!

Glider Wings!

Sonic Alarm!

Cape & Cowl!

ROBIN ROBIN

SPECIES: Robin
BIRTHPLACE: Gotham City
FOOD: Worms

SECRET BIO:
Tim Drake, also known as Robin, trained his pet bird in the art of catching nightcrawlers and named the high-flying hero Robin Robin! This bitty bird soars alongside Batman and the Boy Wonder as the Dynamic Duo fight crime in Gotham City. Like Tim Drake, Robin Robin has a powerful arsenal of weapons, tools, and gadgets.

Bird Brain

High-tech Mask

FLIGHT
Robin Robin is one of the swiftest DC Super-Pets. Former acrobat Tim Drake trained this little bird to be a speedy and skillful flier.

Fireproof Cape

ROBIN SYMBOL & SECRET WEAPON
Robin Robin's symbol is actually a removable, high-tech weapon. These R-shaped throwing stars are similar to Batarangs.

UTILITY BELT
Filled with high-tech gadgets and weapons.

SUPER HERO OWNER
ROBIN
(TIM DRAKE)

ROBIN ROBIN QUOTE!
"The early bird catches the crook!"

ALLIES: **FOES:**

HALEY

Highly Intelligent

GLIDER CAPE
Haley soars through the air with a specially designed cape.

Aerodynamic Suit

Strong Tail

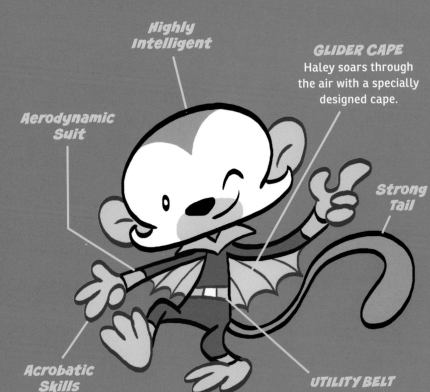

Acrobatic Skills

UTILITY BELT
Filled with high-tech gadgets and weapons.

STATS

SPECIES: Monkey
BIRTHPLACE: Gotham City
FOOD: PB & banana sandwiches

SECRET BIO:
Before becoming a Super-Pet, Haley appeared with his owner, Dick Grayson, also known as Nightwing, at the Haly's Circus. There, he learned his high-flying skills as a showstopping monkey acrobat. When Dick partnered with Batman, Haley followed him. Together, Haley and Nightwing fight crime using their high-flying skills.

BATMAN FAMILY
Haley is part of a group of crime fighters known as the Batman Family. Founded and led by the Dark Knight, the Batman Family teams up to stop Gotham City's worst super-villains, including the Joker, the Penguin, and more!
 Funded by billionaire Bruce Wayne, Batman's civilian identity, the Batman Family uses the Batcave for their headquarters. This secret hideout is located deep below Wayne Manor and contains the Batman Family's weapons, tools, and vehicles.

SUPER HERO OWNER
NIGHTWING

ALLIES: **FOES:**

BATCOW

SPECIES: Cow
BIRTHPLACE: Gotham City
FOOD: Fresh grass

SECRET BIO:
To combat the udder madness in Gotham City, Batgirl taught her cow a few crime-fighting *moo*-ves. The Caped Crusader named her brave bovine Batcow. With an unlimited supply of weapons and gadgets, this heroic heifer is ready to put the city's villains out to pasture.

FUN FACT!
Batcow knows Batgirl's secret identity. She is Barbara Gordon, Commissioner James Gordon's daughter.

BATCOW COWL
Mask protects Batcow's secret identity while allowing plenty of room for chewing cud.

Tuft of Grass

Fireproof Cape

Bat-Symbol

Hard Hooves

What do you call a grumpy cow?
Moo-dy!

UTILITY BELT
This belt holds weapons and gadgets, including smoke pellets.

SUPER HERO OWNER
BATGIRL

ALLIES: **FOES:**

MISTY

STATS

SPECIES: Cat
BIRTHPLACE: Gotham City
FOOD: Soy milk

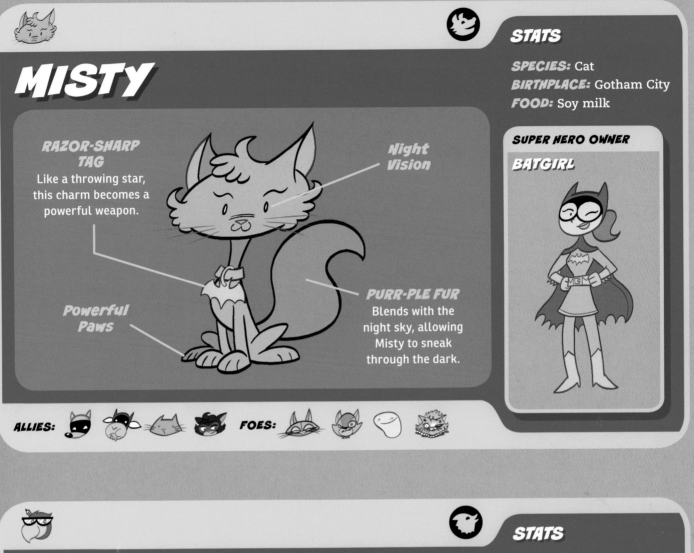

RAZOR-SHARP TAG
Like a throwing star, this charm becomes a powerful weapon.

Night Vision

Powerful Paws

PURR-PLE FUR
Blends with the night sky, allowing Misty to sneak through the dark.

SUPER HERO OWNER
BATGIRL

ALLIES: **FOES:**

CHARLIE

STATS

SPECIES: Parrot
BIRTHPLACE: Gotham City
FOOD: Wheat crackers

HIGHLY INTELLIGENT
Parrots are among the smartest birds on Earth, and Charlie is no exception.

WALKIE-TALKIE
Charlie warns Batgirl of trouble. His voice can travel more than a mile!

Clawed Feet

Brightly Colored Feathers

SUPER HERO OWNER
BATGIRL

ALLIES:    **FOES:**

SHADOW

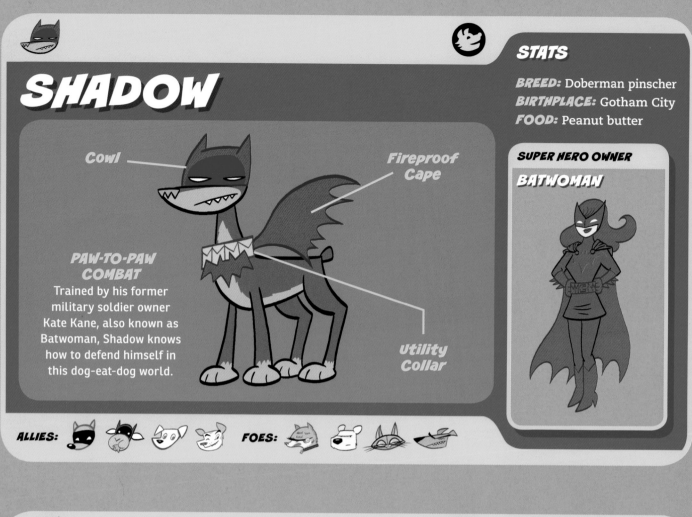

Cowl

Fireproof Cape

PAW-TO-PAW COMBAT
Trained by his former military soldier owner Kate Kane, also known as Batwoman, Shadow knows how to defend himself in this dog-eat-dog world.

Utility Collar

STATS
BREED: Doberman pinscher
BIRTHPLACE: Gotham City
FOOD: Peanut butter

SUPER HERO OWNER
BATWOMAN

ALLIES: FOES:

BLUE

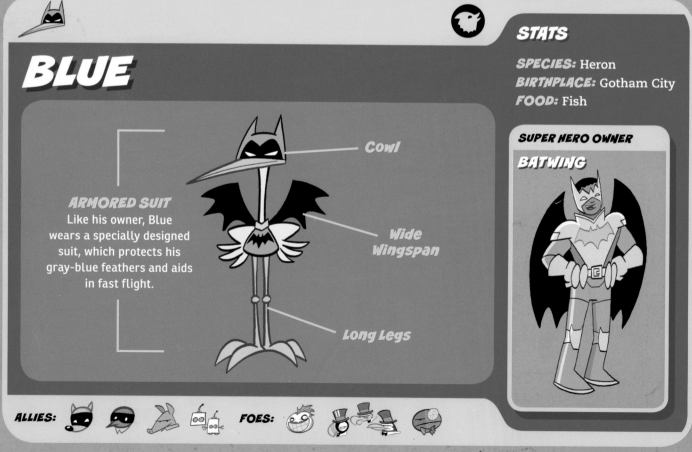

Cowl

ARMORED SUIT
Like his owner, Blue wears a specially designed suit, which protects his gray-blue feathers and aids in fast flight.

Wide Wingspan

Long Legs

STATS
SPECIES: Heron
BIRTHPLACE: Gotham City
FOOD: Fish

SUPER HERO OWNER
BATWING

ALLIES: FOES:

COPPER

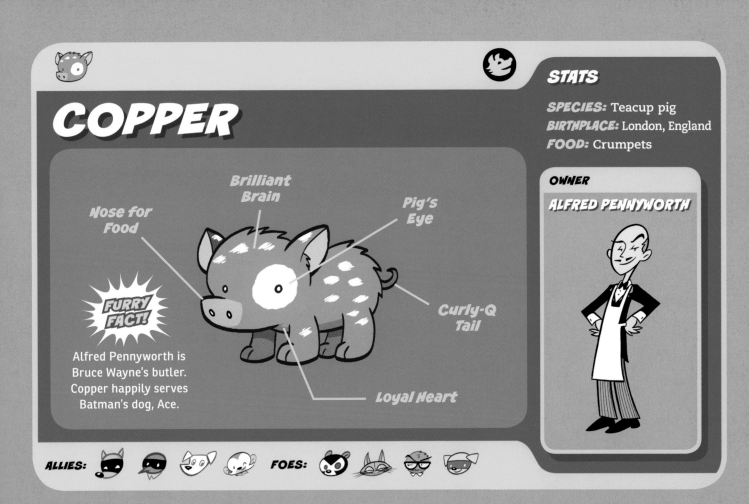

SPECIES: Teacup pig
BIRTHPLACE: London, England
FOOD: Crumpets

Nose for Food

Brilliant Brain

Pig's Eye

Curly-Q Tail

Loyal Heart

FURRY FACT!

Alfred Pennyworth is Bruce Wayne's butler. Copper happily serves Batman's dog, Ace.

OWNER

ALFRED PENNYWORTH

ALLIES: **FOES:**

GUMSHOE

STATS

SPECIES: Aardvark
BIRTHPLACE: Gotham City
FOOD: Termites

Nose for Crime

Thick Skin

Hearty Appetite

Tough Claws

FURRY FACT!

Commissioner Gordon calls Batman with the Bat-Signal. Gumshoe uses a different signal to get Ace's attention: a dog whistle!

OWNER

COMMISSIONER JAMES GORDON

ALLIES: **FOES:**

JUMPA

ROYAL TIARA
Jumpa's royal tiara isn't just fancy headwear. It doubles as a razor-sharp boomerang!

Super Hearing

Golden Necklace

Bracelets of Victory

Superpowered Tail

Handy Pouch

SPEEDY STEED
Lightning-quick legs make Jumpa a speedy ride for Wonder Woman.

What's a kangaroo's favorite season? **Spring!**

STATS

SPECIES: Kanga
BIRTHPLACE: Paradise Island
FOOD: Jumping beans

SECRET BIO:
Kangas are found only on Paradise Island (*see page 33*). Like kangaroos, kangas can leap long distances, but they're also super-speedy. These heroic hoppers are the royal rides of Wonder Woman and other Amazons. Jumpa carries royal weapons in her pouch, including a royal tiara, silver bracelets, and the Lasso of Truth.

WEAKNESS:
Bracelets of Submission

SUPER HERO OWNER
WONDER WOMAN

ALLIES: **FOES:**

LEEPA

Golden Necklace

Quick Tail

Small Size

Lightning-fast Feet

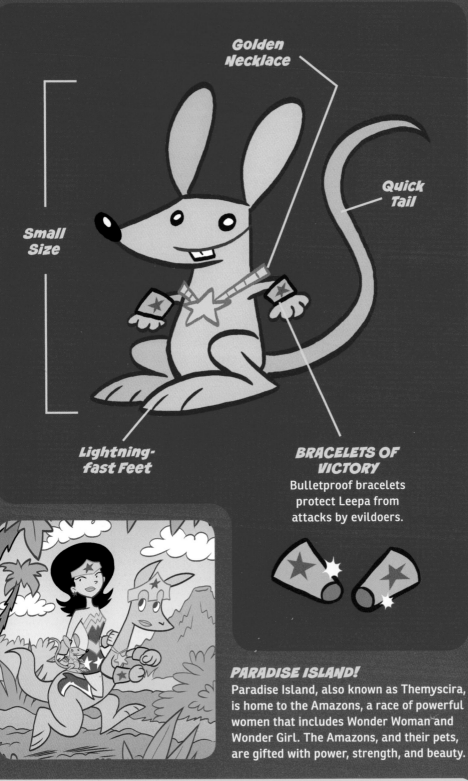

BRACELETS OF VICTORY
Bulletproof bracelets protect Leepa from attacks by evildoers.

PARADISE ISLAND!
Paradise Island, also known as Themyscira, is home to the Amazons, a race of powerful women that includes Wonder Woman and Wonder Girl. The Amazons, and their pets, are gifted with power, strength, and beauty.

STATS

SPECIES:
Kanga mouse
BIRTHPLACE:
Paradise Island
FOOD: Cheddar cheese

SECRET BIO:
Kanga mice are bred on Paradise Island as playmates for the larger kangas. These little wonders have the same powers as their full-sized friends, as well as a psychic connection to them. When Wonder Girl is in danger of being defeated, Leepa does not hesitate to help her owner squeak out a victory!

WEAKNESS:
Bracelets of Submission

SUPER HERO OWNER
WONDER GIRL

ALLIES: **FOES:**

STORM

MIND COMMUNICATION
Like his owner, Storm speaks with other sea-life using only his mind.

Ultra Smart

Underwater Breathing

Aqua Belt

HORSEPOWER
As Aquaman's trusty steed, Storm is a tsunami-quick swimmer. This seahorse packs enough horsepower to leave villains in his wake.

STATS

SPECIES: Seahorse
BIRTHPLACE: Atlantis
FOOD:
Shrimp and seaweed

SECRET BIO:
When Aquaman needs a lift, he calls his superpowered seahorse. With the Sea King on his back, Storm can sail beneath the sea or ride atop the waves at super-speed. He's a pretty good dancer, too! With Storm's help, the city of Atlantis will never be lost again!

WEAKNESS:
Lack of water

SUPER HERO OWNER

AQUAMAN

SALTY THE AQUADOG

SPECIES:
Golden retriever
BIRTHPLACE:
Coast City
FOOD:
Saltwater taffy

SECRET BIO:
Storm might be Aquaman's loyal underwater steed, but Salty is the Sea King's best friend on dry land!

ALLIES: **FOES:**

TOPO

STATS

SPECIES: Octopus
BIRTHPLACE: Atlantis
FOOD: Prawns

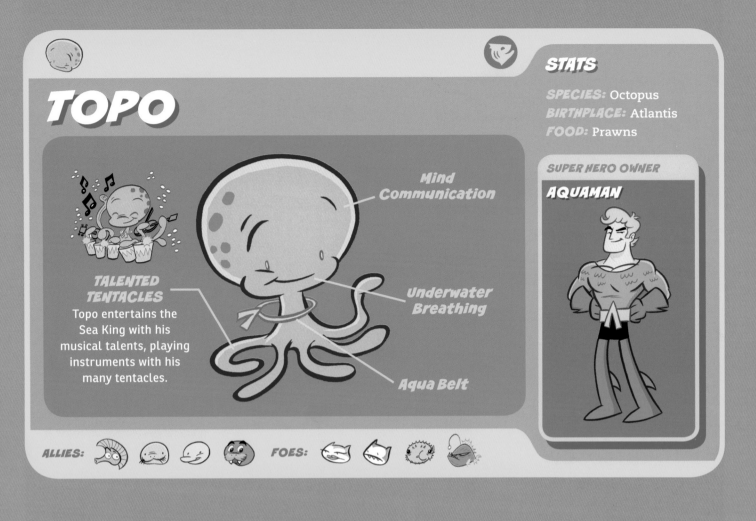

Mind Communication

TALENTED TENTACLES
Topo entertains the Sea King with his musical talents, playing instruments with his many tentacles.

Underwater Breathing

Aqua Belt

SUPER HERO OWNER
AQUAMAN

ALLIES: FOES:

ARK

STATS

SPECIES: Seal
BIRTHPLACE: Atlantis
FOOD: Fish

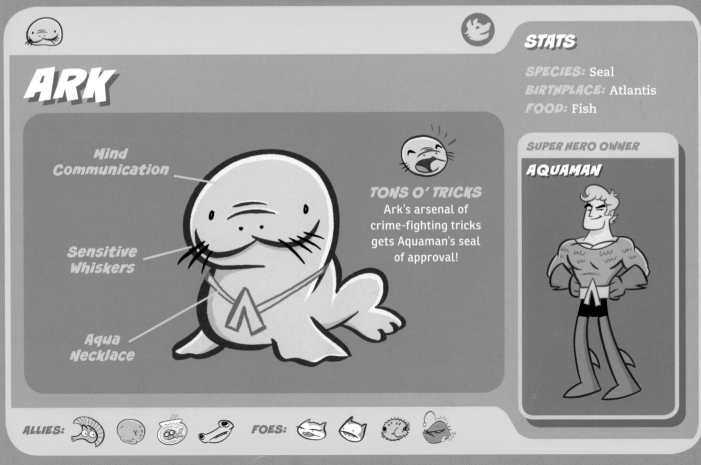

Mind Communication

Sensitive Whiskers

Aqua Necklace

TONS O' TRICKS
Ark's arsenal of crime-fighting tricks gets Aquaman's seal of approval!

SUPER HERO OWNER
AQUAMAN

ALLIES: FOES:

TUSKY

STATS

SPECIES: Walrus
BIRTHPLACE: Atlantis
FOOD: Mollusks

Sea Smarts

Extra Large Tusks

Aqua Necklace

DARING DIVER
As a mammal, Tusky must breathe fresh air. But this fearless walrus will dive to the deepest depths on a single gulp of air.

SUPER HERO OWNER

AQUALAD

ALLIES: **FOES:**

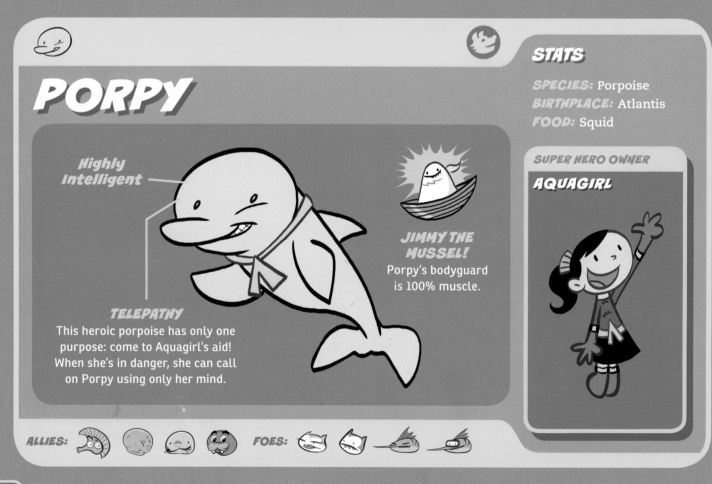

PORPY

STATS

SPECIES: Porpoise
BIRTHPLACE: Atlantis
FOOD: Squid

Highly Intelligent

JIMMY THE MUSSEL!
Porpy's bodyguard is 100% muscle.

TELEPATHY
This heroic porpoise has only one purpose: come to Aquagirl's aid! When she's in danger, she can call on Porpy using only her mind.

SUPER HERO OWNER

AQUAGIRL

ALLIES: **FOES:**

FLUFFY

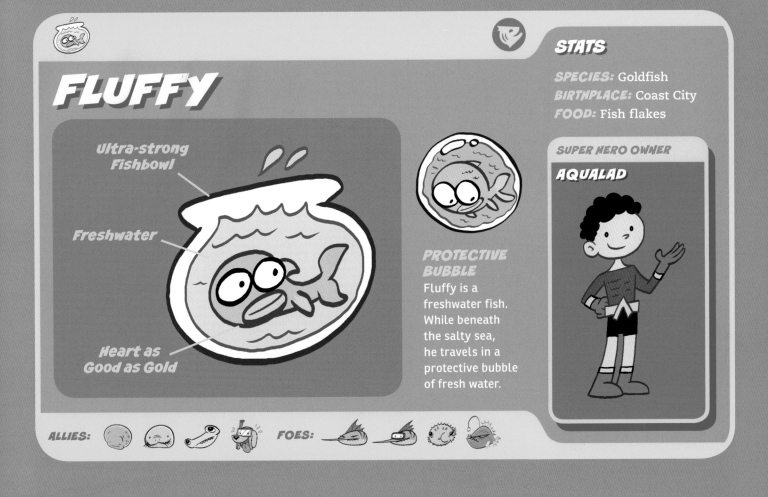

- **Ultra-strong Fishbowl**
- **Freshwater**
- **Heart as Good as Gold**

PROTECTIVE BUBBLE
Fluffy is a freshwater fish. While beneath the salty sea, he travels in a protective bubble of fresh water.

STATS
SPECIES: Goldfish
BIRTHPLACE: Coast City
FOOD: Fish flakes

SUPER HERO OWNER
AQUALAD

ALLIES: **FOES:**

GEOFFREY

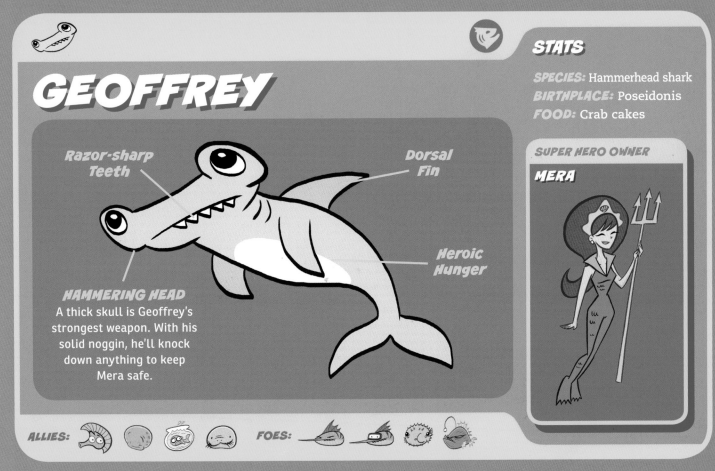

- **Razor-sharp Teeth**
- **Dorsal Fin**
- **Heroic Hunger**

HAMMERING HEAD
A thick skull is Geoffrey's strongest weapon. With his solid noggin, he'll knock down anything to keep Mera safe.

STATS
SPECIES: Hammerhead shark
BIRTHPLACE: Poseidonis
FOOD: Crab cakes

SUPER HERO OWNER
MERA

ALLIES: **FOES:**

WHATZIT

SECRET BIO:
Merton McSnurtle has followed in the fast and furious footsteps of the World's Greatest Speedsters, including his current owner, Barry Allen. As the Fastest Turtle Alive, Merton helps keep Central City safe from evil pets, including his iciest enemy, Admiral Peary (*see page* 105).

ALIASES:
The Fastest Turtle Alive
The Scarlet Shell
The Merton of Motion
The Terrapin of Speed

SLEEK UNIFORM
Merton stores his uniform inside a high-tech ring. The suit protects the Fastest Turtle Alive from high-speed dangers.

Quick Wits

Strong Shell

Speedy Reflexes

Super Metabolism

SUPER-SPEED
With super-speed, Whatzit can create tornadoes, vibrate his molecules to pass through solid objects, and, of course, run crazy fast!

Where does a turtle go in a storm?

A SHELL-ter!

SUPER HERO OWNER

THE FLASH

ALLIES: **FOES:**

F.E.L.I.X.

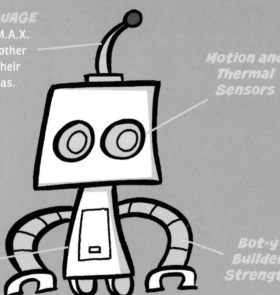

COMPUTER LANGUAGE
Both F.E.L.I.X. and M.A.X. communicate with other computers using their high-tech antennas.

Motion and Thermal Sensors

Rustproof Body

Bot-y Builder Strength

SPECIES: Robots
BIRTHPLACE: San Francisco
FOOD: Nuts and bolts

SECRET BIO:
Cyborg, also known as Victor Stone, is half human and half robot. Although this super hero has many human friends, he had very few robot ones. So he built them! With dozens of specialized gadgets, protective armor, and digital brains, F.E.L.I.X. and M.A.X. are high-tech Super-Pets. Or, as some would say, they are two computer chips off the old block!

WEAKNESSES:
Water
Battery life

M.A.X.

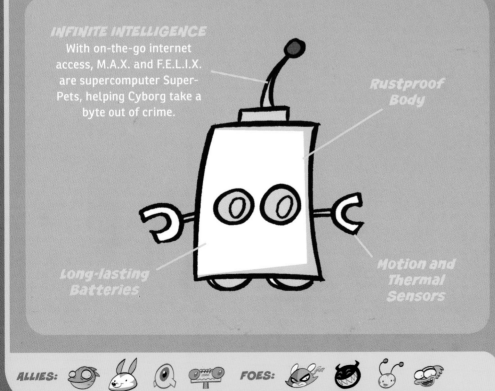

INFINITE INTELLIGENCE
With on-the-go internet access, M.A.X. and F.E.L.I.X. are supercomputer Super-Pets, helping Cyborg take a byte out of crime.

Rustproof Body

Long-lasting Batteries

Motion and Thermal Sensors

SUPER HERO OWNER

CYBORG

 **ALLIES:** **FOES:**

B'DG
Green Lantern, Space Sector 1014

STATS

SPECIES: Space squirrel
BIRTHPLACE: H'lven
FOOD: Ch'ps and salsa

SECRET BIO:
Like all members of the Green Lantern Corps, B'dg was chosen to protect an area of space from evil. He is pals with fellow Green Lantern Hal Jordan—not his pet! Like all Green Lantern members, B'dg follows a sacred oath:

"In brightest day, in blackest night, no evil shall escape my sight. Let those who worship evil's might, beware my power, Green Lantern's Light!"

POWER RING
Like all Green Lanterns, B'dg wears a green power ring, which is fueled by his own willpower. The ring has many uses:

Creates Anything Imaginable

Enables Flight

Powers Force Fields

DC SUPER-PETS TRIBUTE!
B'dg wasn't the first Green Lantern of Sector 1014. Before him, another space rodent protected the area: Ch'p, also from H'lven! Trained by the Green Lanterns Kilowog and Hal Jordan, Ch'p served heroically for many years.

SUPER HERO PAL

HAL JORDAN
Green Lantern, Space Sector 2814

ALLIES: **FOES:**

BZZD
Green Lantern, Space Sector 2261

SPECIES: Space fly
BIRTHPLACE: Apiaton
FOOD: Regurgitated space garbage

SECRET BIO:
As a young larva on Apiaton, located in Space Sector 2261, Bzzd watched space pirates take over his home planet. Later, he joined the Green Lantern Corps to defeat evildoers throughout the universe. Like all Green Lanterns, Bzzd wields a green power ring. He is also the leader of the Green Lantern Bug Corps, a powerful posse of space insects (see page 42).

FUN FACT!
Bzzd's favorite sport is baseball!

STINGER
Bzzd's stinger contains a powerful venom!

Winged Flight

FUN FACT!

PALS, NOT PETS!
All Green Lanterns—no matter what shape, size, or species—are official members of the Green Lantern Corps and *not* pets!

What do you call a fly with no wings?

A walk!

POWER RING
With his unmatched willpower, Bzzd creates anything imaginable from his power ring.

SUPER HERO PAL

JOHN STEWART
Green Lantern, Space Sector 2814

ALLIES: **FOES:**

41

GREEN LANTERN BUG CORPS
Green Lanterns, Headquarters Space Sector 2261

BZZD (LEADER)

SPECIES: Fly
POWER: Power ring; stinger
FOOD: Regurgitated space garbage

EENY

SPECIES: Ant
POWER: Power ring; strength
FOOD: Space plants

BUZZOO

SPECIES: Bee
POWER: Power ring; stinger
FOOD: Space nectar

BATTLING BUGS!

The Green Lantern Bug Corps fear no one! Even their peskiest pests, the Sinestro Bug Corps (*see page* 106) is no match for these battle bugs.

FOSSFUR

SPECIES: Firefly
POWER: Power ring; glow butt
FOOD: Space slugs

ALLIES: **FOES:**

STATS

BIO:

With their superpowered rings, the Green Lantern Bug Corps guard the universe and protect it from evil. They are led by Bzzd, the fiercest fly in the universe.

POWER RINGS!

Like all Green Lanterns, the Green Lantern Bug Corps wear green power rings, which are fueled by their own willpower and can generate any form imaginable!

SUPER HERO PAL

MEDPHYLL
Green Lantern,
Space Sector 1287

GRATCH
SPECIES: Grasshopper
POWER: Power ring; hops
FOOD: Space leaves

ZHOOMP
SPECIES: Mantis
POWER: Power ring; faith
FOOD: Space insects

G'NORT
Green Lantern, Space Sector 2814

POWER RING
Green power rings are fueled by unmatched willpower. The ring has many uses:

Creates Anything Imaginable

Enables Flight

Powers Force Fields

SECRET BIO:
Born on the planet G'newt, young G'nort tried to concentrate on schoolwork, but he always spaced out—literally! He wanted to fly through the galaxy as a member of the Green Lantern Corps. Eventually, his dog dream came true, and G'nort became a protector of the universe, wielding his green power ring against the Sinestro Corps.

FUN FACT!
G'nort's full name is G'nort Esplanade G'neeshmacher!

SUPER HERO PAL

GUY GARDNER
Green Lantern, Space Sector 2814

POWER RINGS!
There are many Lantern Corps throughout the universe—each with a different colored ring:

RED LANTERN
Fueled by rage

GREEN LANTERN
Fueled by willpower

STAR SAPPHIRE
Fueled by love

ORANGE LANTERN
Fueled by avarice

BLUE LANTERN
Fueled by hope

BLACK LANTERN
Fueled by death

YELLOW LANTERN
Fueled by fear

INDIGO TRIBE
Fueled by compassion

WHITE LANTERN
Fueled by life

ALLIES: **FOES:**

ZALLION
Green Lantern, Space Sector 2814

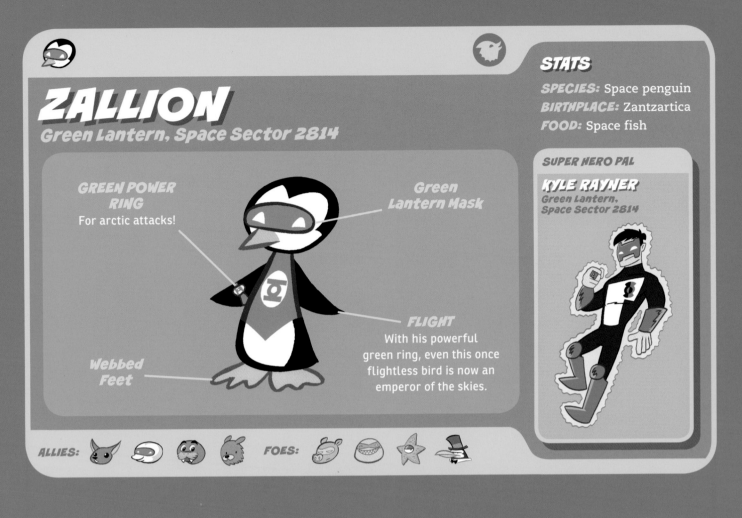

GREEN POWER RING
For arctic attacks!

Green Lantern Mask

Webbed Feet

FLIGHT
With his powerful green ring, even this once flightless bird is now an emperor of the skies.

STATS
SPECIES: Space penguin
BIRTHPLACE: Zantzartica
FOOD: Space fish

SUPER HERO PAL
KYLE RAYNER
Green Lantern, Space Sector 2814

ALLIES: **FOES:**

STRIPEZOID
Green Lantern, Space Sector 0674

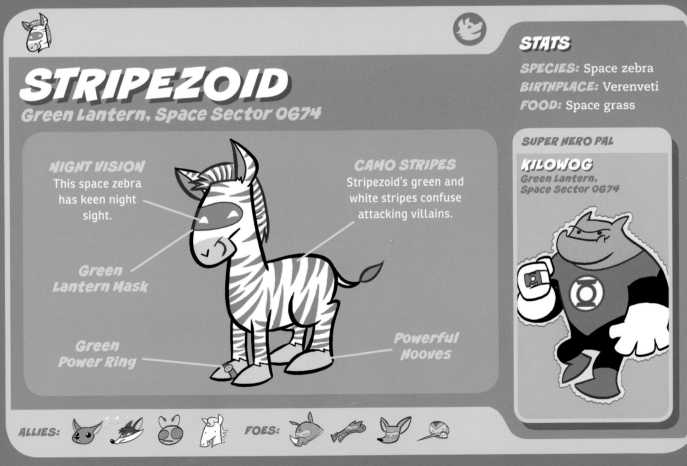

NIGHT VISION
This space zebra has keen night sight.

Green Lantern Mask

Green Power Ring

CAMO STRIPES
Stripezoid's green and white stripes confuse attacking villains.

Powerful Hooves

STATS
SPECIES: Space zebra
BIRTHPLACE: Verenveti
FOOD: Space grass

SUPER HERO PAL
KILOWOG
Green Lantern, Space Sector 0674

ALLIES: **FOES:**

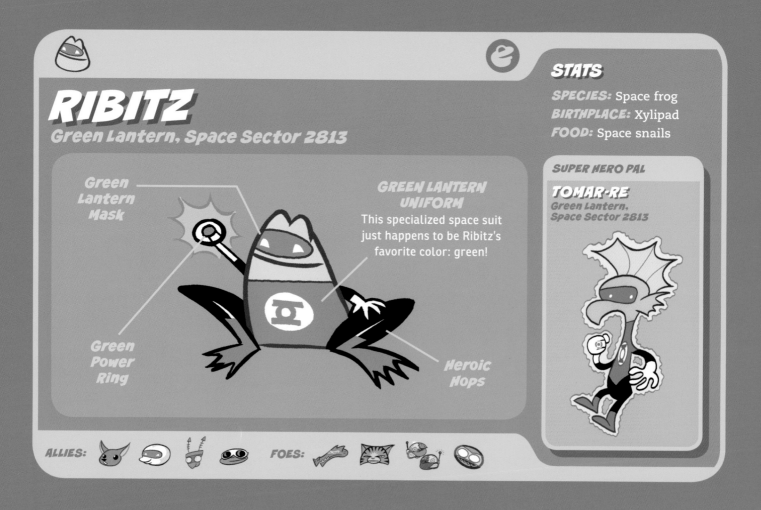

RIBITZ
Green Lantern, Space Sector 2813

Green Lantern Mask

GREEN LANTERN UNIFORM
This specialized space suit just happens to be Ribitz's favorite color: green!

Green Power Ring

Heroic Hops

STATS
SPECIES: Space frog
BIRTHPLACE: Xylipad
FOOD: Space snails

SUPER HERO PAL
TOMAR-RE
Green Lantern, Space Sector 2813

ALLIES: **FOES:**

SEN-TAG
Green Lantern, Space Sector 1418

Green Power Ring

CLEVER
Like a fox!

Green Lantern Uniform

FUN FACT!
Green Lanterns are chosen by a group called the Guardians of the Universe from the planet Oa.

STATS
SPECIES: Humanoid fox
BIRTHPLACE: Zuriozz
FOOD: Space mice

SUPER HERO PAL
SALAAK
Green Lantern, Space Sector 1418

ALLIES: **FOES:**

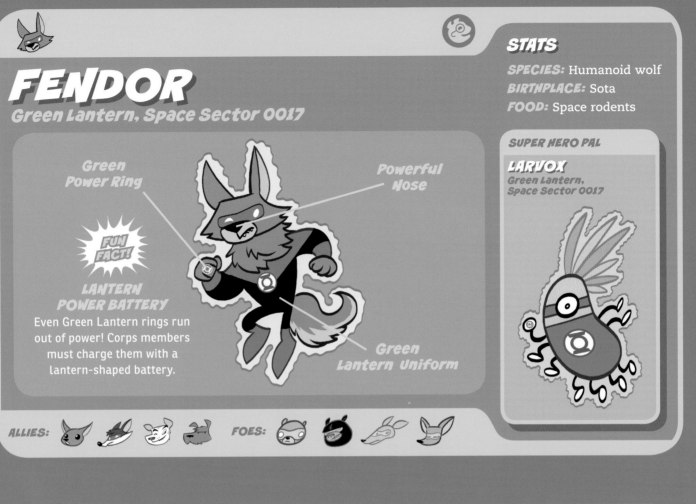

FENDOR
Green Lantern, Space Sector 0017

STATS
SPECIES: Humanoid wolf
BIRTHPLACE: Sota
FOOD: Space rodents

Green Power Ring

Powerful Nose

FUN FACT!

LANTERN POWER BATTERY
Even Green Lantern rings run out of power! Corps members must charge them with a lantern-shaped battery.

Green Lantern Uniform

SUPER HERO PAL
LARVOX
Green Lantern, Space Sector 0017

ALLIES: **FOES:**

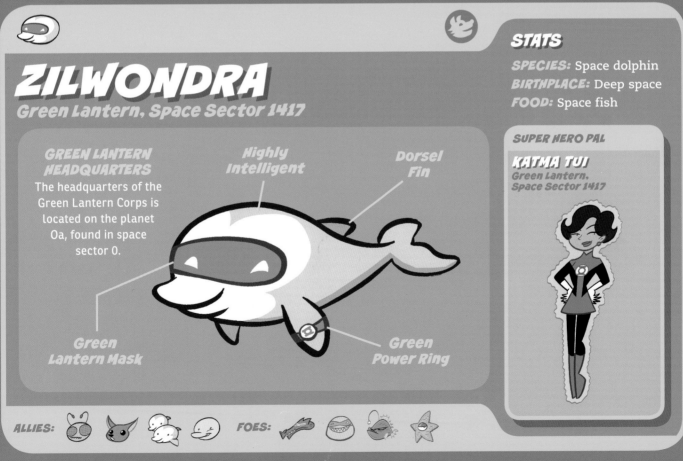

ZILWONDRA
Green Lantern, Space Sector 1417

STATS
SPECIES: Space dolphin
BIRTHPLACE: Deep space
FOOD: Space fish

GREEN LANTERN HEADQUARTERS
The headquarters of the Green Lantern Corps is located on the planet Oa, found in space sector 0.

Highly Intelligent

Dorsel Fin

Green Lantern Mask

Green Power Ring

SUPER HERO PAL
KATMA TUI
Green Lantern, Space Sector 1417

ALLIES: **FOES:**

ZOOK

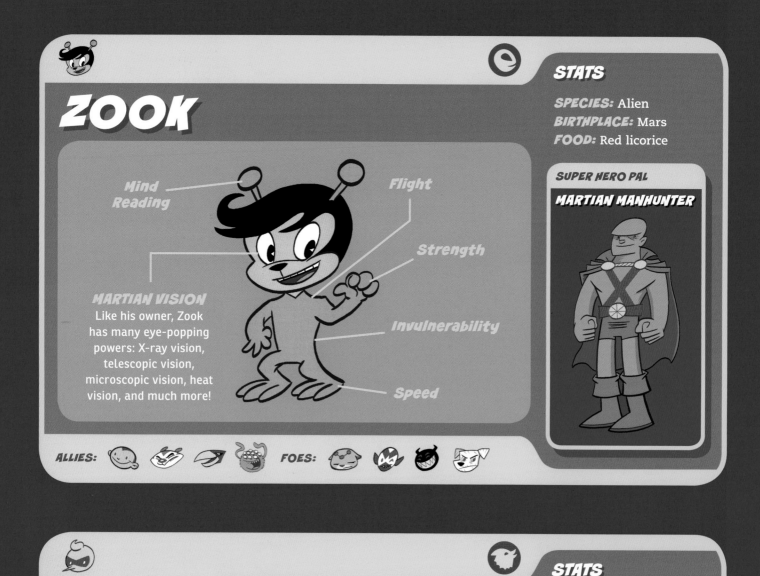

Mind Reading

Flight

Strength

Invulnerability

Speed

MARTIAN VISION
Like his owner, Zook has many eye-popping powers: X-ray vision, telescopic vision, microscopic vision, heat vision, and much more!

STATS
SPECIES: Alien
BIRTHPLACE: Mars
FOOD: Red licorice

SUPER HERO PAL
MARTIAN MANHUNTER

ALLIES: **FOES:**

PIERCE

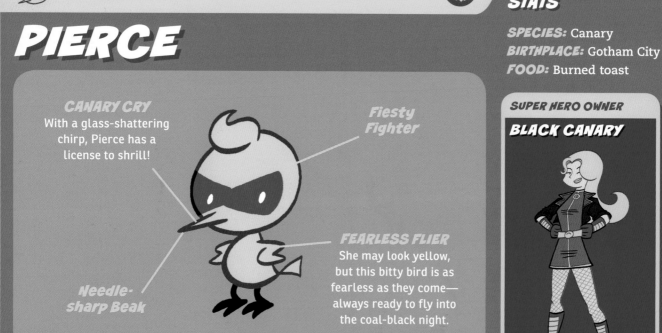

CANARY CRY
With a glass-shattering chirp, Pierce has a license to shrill!

Fiesty Fighter

Needle-Sharp Beak

FEARLESS FLIER
She may look yellow, but this bitty bird is as fearless as they come—always ready to fly into the coal-black night.

STATS
SPECIES: Canary
BIRTHPLACE: Gotham City
FOOD: Burned toast

SUPER HERO OWNER
BLACK CANARY

ALLIES: **FOES:**

QUIVER

Feathered Cap

Custom Bow

ARCHERY SKILLS
With a specially designed bow and high-tech arrows, Quiver aims to take down his *arch*-enemies.

Quiver of Arrows

Razor-sharp Quills

SUPER HERO OWNER

GREEN ARROW

ALLIES: FOES:

QUILL

STATS

SPECIES: Porcupine
BIRTHPLACE: Star City
FOOD: Fondue

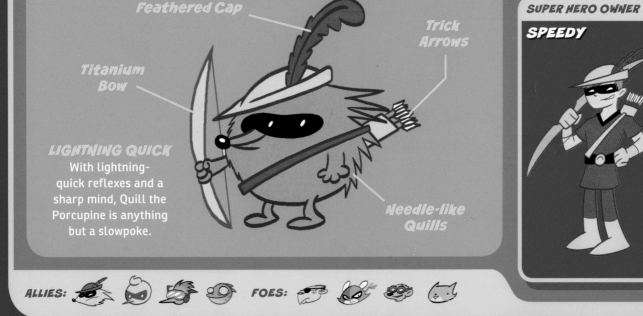

Feathered Cap

Trick Arrows

Titanium Bow

LIGHTNING QUICK
With lightning-quick reflexes and a sharp mind, Quill the Porcupine is anything but a slowpoke.

Needle-like Quills

SUPER HERO OWNER

SPEEDY

ALLIES: FOES:

HOPPY

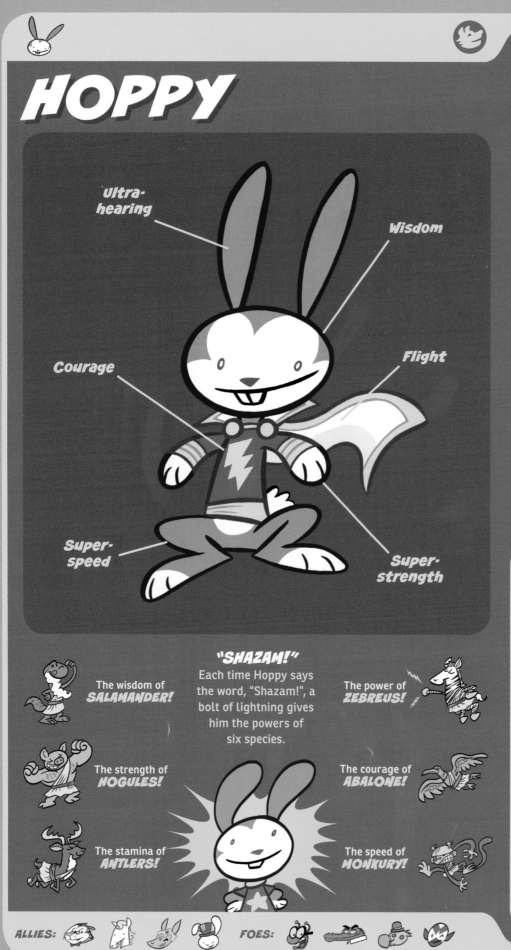

Ultra-hearing

Wisdom

Courage

Flight

Super-speed

Super-strength

"SHAZAM!"
Each time Hoppy says the word, "Shazam!", a bolt of lightning gives him the powers of six species.

The wisdom of **SALAMANDER!**

The power of **ZEBREUS!**

The strength of **HOGULES!**

The courage of **ABALONE!**

The stamina of **ANTLERS!**

The speed of **MONKURY!**

SECRET BIO:
One day in the town of Animalville, a regular rabbit named Hoppy wanted to be like his favorite super hero, Shazam!. He spoke the hero's magic word, "Shazam!", and Hoppy gained superpowers himself. With the powers of six species, Hoppy is one of the universe's most heroic hares!

FUN FACT!
Even Hoppy's best friend, Millie, doesn't know his secret hero identity.

SUPER HERO OWNER
SHAZAM!

ALLIES: **FOES:**

TAWKY TAWNY

STATS

SPECIES: Tiger
BIRTHPLACE: India
FOOD: Filet mignon

SECRET BIO:
Born in the jungles of India, Mr. Tawky Tawny grew to become much more than a tiger in a snappy suit. He is super-intelligent and a loyal friend to Hoppy, Freddy, Mary, and Shazam! Although Tawky Tawny has the strength of a ferocious tiger, he is really a peaceful pussycat at heart.

FUN FACT!
Tawky Tawny has the strange ability to transform into an armored smilodon!

Always On Time

Super-smart

Snappy Dresser

Strong Tail

STRENGTH
Tawky Tawny uses his incredible tiger-like strength to help Hoppy wrap up members of the Monster Society of Evil!

SHAZAM!... THE WIZARD
Shazam! is a 3000-year-old Egyptian wizard who gave young Billy Batson the power to transform into the mighty super hero Shazam!.

SUPER HERO PALS
FREDDY & MARY

ALLIES: **FOES:**

SPOT

SPEEDY TRAVEL
At microscopic size, Spot and his owner, the Atom, travel through cable and phone lines. Talk about telecommuting!

Brilliant Mind

Bitty Bark

Tiny Tail

Giant Heart

Why are dalmatians no good at Hide and Seek?
They're always spotted!

Mini Mutt!
With their high-tech suits, Spot and his owner can shrink to many different sizes. However, even when he's the size of an ant, the mini mutt maintains his full-sized strength, making him one powerful pup!

STATS

SPECIES: Dog
BIRTHPLACE: Ivy Town
FOOD: Mini pumpkins

SECRET BIO:
Spot helped his master, Dr. Ray Palmer, develop a shrinking machine using the dust of a white dwarf star. After perfecting the invention, the duo developed two high-tech shrinking suits, and this common canine became the mighty mite, Spot! His master became a microscopic super hero, too: the Atom! Together, this puny pair use their antlike abilities to take down big-time baddies.

SUPER HERO OWNER
THE ATOM

ALLIES: **FOES:**

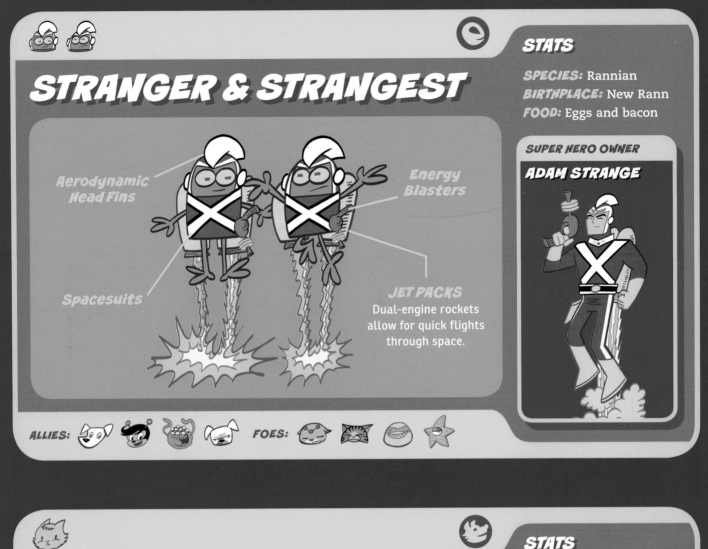

STRANGER & STRANGEST

Aerodynamic Head Fins

Spacesuits

Energy Blasters

JET PACKS
Dual-engine rockets allow for quick flights through space.

STATS

SPECIES: Rannian
BIRTHPLACE: New Rann
FOOD: Eggs and bacon

SUPER HERO OWNER
ADAM STRANGE

ALLIES: **FOES:**

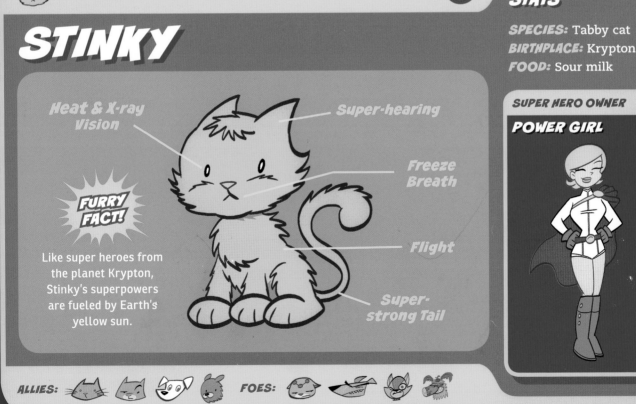

STINKY

Heat & X-ray Vision

Super-hearing

FURRY FACT!

Like super heroes from the planet Krypton, Stinky's superpowers are fueled by Earth's yellow sun.

Freeze Breath

Flight

Super-strong Tail

STATS

SPECIES: Tabby cat
BIRTHPLACE: Krypton
FOOD: Sour milk

SUPER HERO OWNER
POWER GIRL

ALLIES: **FOES:**

TIBBAR

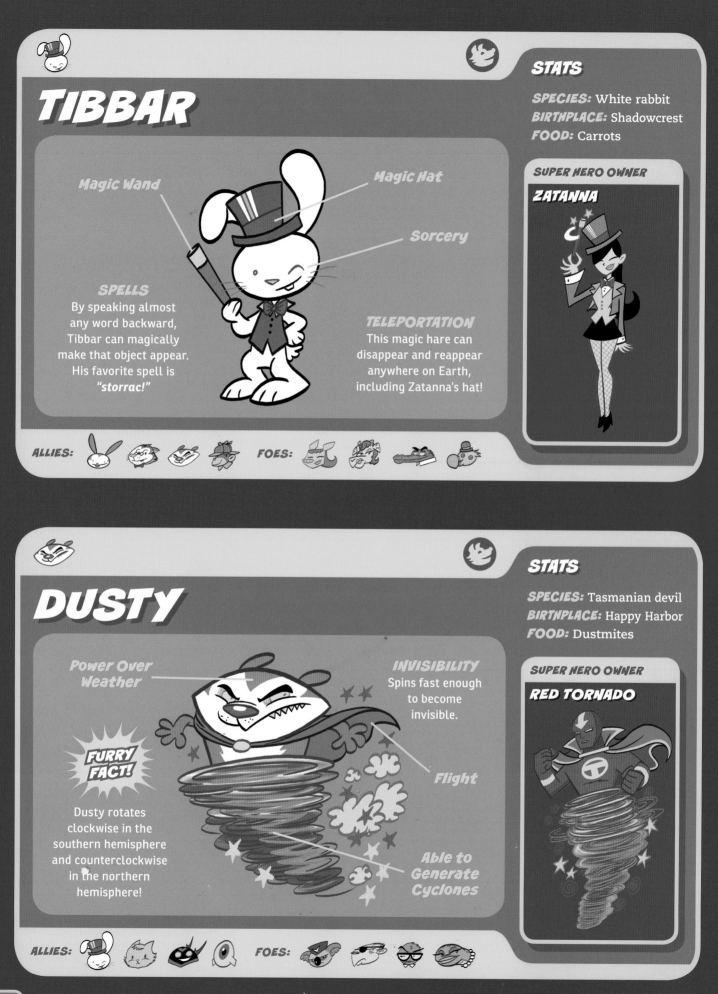

Magic Wand

Magic Hat

Sorcery

SPELLS
By speaking almost any word backward, Tibbar can magically make that object appear. His favorite spell is *"storrac!"*

TELEPORTATION
This magic hare can disappear and reappear anywhere on Earth, including Zatanna's hat!

STATS
SPECIES: White rabbit
BIRTHPLACE: Shadowcrest
FOOD: Carrots

SUPER HERO OWNER
ZATANNA

ALLIES: **FOES:**

DUSTY

Power Over Weather

INVISIBILITY
Spins fast enough to become invisible.

FURRY FACT!
Dusty rotates clockwise in the southern hemisphere and counterclockwise in the northern hemisphere!

Flight

Able to Generate Cyclones

STATS
SPECIES: Tasmanian devil
BIRTHPLACE: Happy Harbor
FOOD: Dustmites

SUPER HERO OWNER
RED TORNADO

ALLIES: **FOES:**

PLASTIC FROG

STATS

SPECIES: Flexy Frog
BIRTHPLACE: Costa Tico
FOOD: Fruit Flies

SECRET BIO:
One day, during a tropical storm, Plastic Frog climbed up a very tall tree. A rubber tree. Suddenly, a bolt of lightning sizzled through the air. The bolt struck the rubber tree. Somehow, the lightning, the rubber, and the little frog's slimy skin all got mixed up together. Ever since that day, Plastic Frog has been able to stretch his body to amazing lengths! As soon as he met Plastic Man, the two of them started fighting crime together.

FLEXY FLIGHT?
Although he can't fly, Plastic Frog can stretch his body into a sail, allowing him to float on a breeze.

SUNGLASSES
Protect against UV rays.

Funny

FLEXY SIGHT
Plastic Frog can stretch his eyes to see for miles, down holes, or even around corners!

FANTASTIC FLEXY FROG!
A rubber tree accident gave Plastic Frog the power to streeeeetch!

What is a frog's favorite game?

Leap frog!

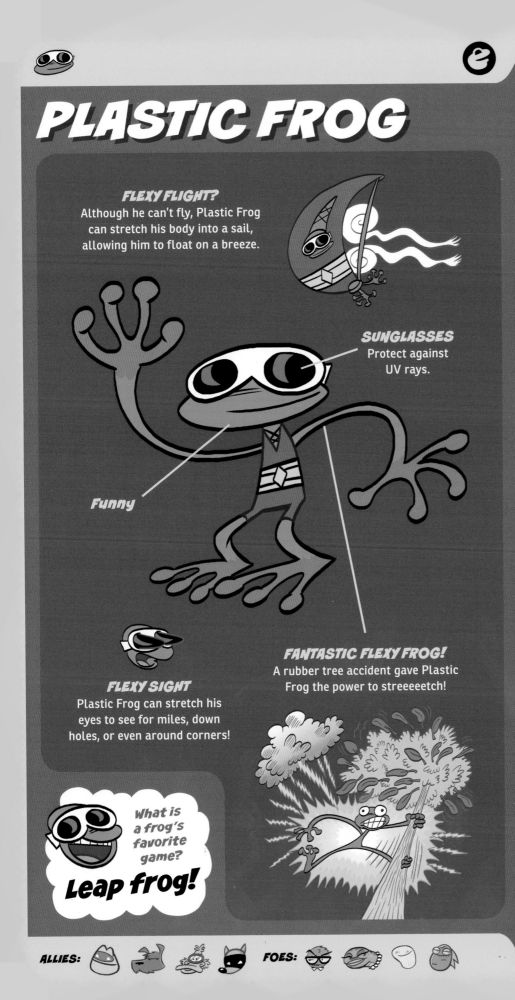

SUPER HERO OWNER
PLASTIC MAN

ALLIES: **FOES:**

BIG TED

Nth METAL HARNESS
Found only on the planet Thanagar, Nth Metal allows wearers to fly through space and heal quickly, as well as increasing the strength of anything it touches.

HAWK'S EYE
Ultra-sharp eyesight!

Speedy Flight

Sharp Talons

SECRET BIO:
Since hatching from an egg on the planet Thanagar, Big Ted has helped his high-flying owners catch their prey. Like all Thanagarians, Big Ted has the naturally keen and quick powers of a hawk, which are greatly enhanced by his Nth Metal Harness.

FURRY FACT!
Bird-brained? Not quite. Big Ted is capable of planning complicated crime-fighting attacks on the fly.

THE HAWKSHIP!

Big Ted copilots the Hawkship, a specially designed spaceship able to fly through the galaxy at supersonic speeds. The Hawkship is constructed from Nth Metal and is heavily equipped with weapons for fighting intergalactic villains!

SUPER HERO OWNERS

HAWKMAN & HAWKWOMAN

ALLIES: **FOES:**

SCARABIAN KNIGHT

STATS

SPECIES: Scarab beetle
BIRTHPLACE: El Paso, Texas
FOOD: Grubs

Energy Absorber

Flight

Pincers

BUG BITE!
When Scarabian Knight attaches to a person, the person takes on this bug's abilities. That's one powerful bite!

SUPER HERO OWNER
BLUE BEETLE

ALLIES: **FOES:**

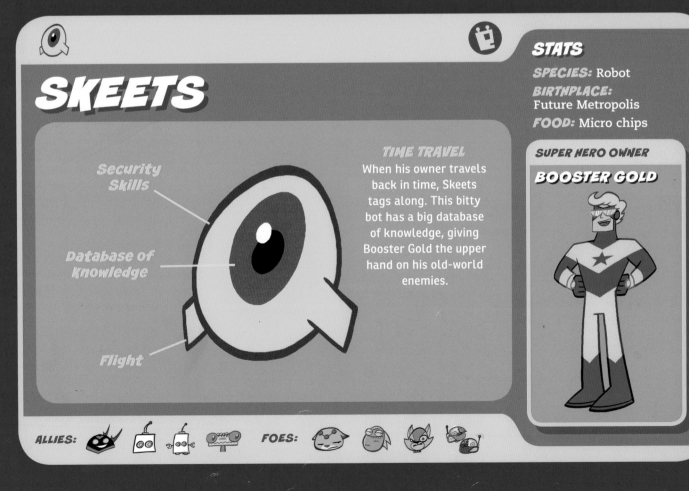

SKEETS

STATS

SPECIES: Robot
BIRTHPLACE: Future Metropolis
FOOD: Micro chips

Security Skills

Database of Knowledge

Flight

TIME TRAVEL
When his owner travels back in time, Skeets tags along. This bitty bot has a big database of knowledge, giving Booster Gold the upper hand on his old-world enemies.

SUPER HERO OWNER
BOOSTER GOLD

ALLIES: **FOES:**

DETECTIVE CHIMP

STATS

SPECIES: Chimpanzee
BIRTHPLACE: Africa
FOOD: Figs

Able to Speak to All Animals

Genius Intelligence

Detective Skills

Strength

FURRY FACT!

Detective Chimp's real name is Bobo T. Chimpanzee!

SUPER HERO PAL

ELONGATED MAN

ALLIES: FOES:

REX THE WONDER DOG

STATS

SPECIES: Dog
BIRTHPLACE: U.S.A.
FOOD: Rawhide

Highly Intelligent

LOYAL SERVICE
Rex is a real-life service dog—military service! He led the U.S. Army's K-9 Corps during World War II.

Sensitive Snout

Powerful Tail

Ruff & Tough

SUPER HERO OWNER

SGT. ROCK

ALLIES: FOES:

KING

STATS

SPECIES: Lion
BIRTHPLACE: Africa
FOOD: Cheeseburgers

Communicates with All Animals

King of the Jungle

Strength

LION PRIDE
When King says catching crooks is "no big thing," this lion is lyin'. He takes pride in catching his prey.

Powerful Tail

SUPER HERO OWNER

ANIMAL MAN

ALLIES: **FOES:**

CHARLIE

STATS

SPECIES: Owl
BIRTHPLACE: Portsmouth City, Oregon
FOOD: Rodents

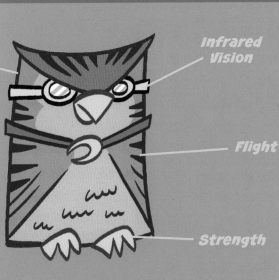

360 Degrees Head Rotation

Infrared Vision

Flight

NIGHT OWL
When the sun sets, Charlie rises. This owl doesn't give a hoot about sleep! He won't rest until he finds out hoo-hoo-dunit.

Strength

SUPER HERO OWNER

DOCTOR MID-NITE

ALLIES: **FOES:**

DOOM PET PATROL

LINC
BREED: Dachsund
POWER: Stretchy; size manipulation
FOOD: Bubble gum

INTELLO

SPECIES: Platypus
POWER: Telepathy
FOOD: Insect larvae

DOOM PATROL

SUPER HERO OWNER
ELASTI-GIRL

SUPER HERO OWNER
MENTO

ALLIES: FOES:

BIO:
The Doom Patrol were considered misfits and freaks because of their unusual powers. But they were turned into a powerful team by a wheelchair-bound mastermind, known as Chief, and they found success together combating evil throughout the world and beyond. Their pets, the Doom Pet Patrol, found pride and purpose by partnering up and pitching in to rescue folks from robbers, rogues, and rotten rascals.

ANTI-MATT

SPECIES: Mouse
POWER: Flight; ability to generate explosions
FOOD: Currant jelly

SHELLY

SPECIES: Armadillo
POWER: Superhuman strength; endurance; speed; vision; armor
FOOD: Agave

FUN FACT!

Beast Boy and Bumblebee (*see pages 63 & 64*) have also been members of the Doom Patrol.

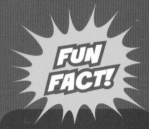

SUPER HERO OWNER
NEGATIVE MAN

SUPER HERO OWNER
ROBOTMAN

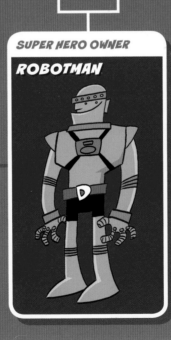

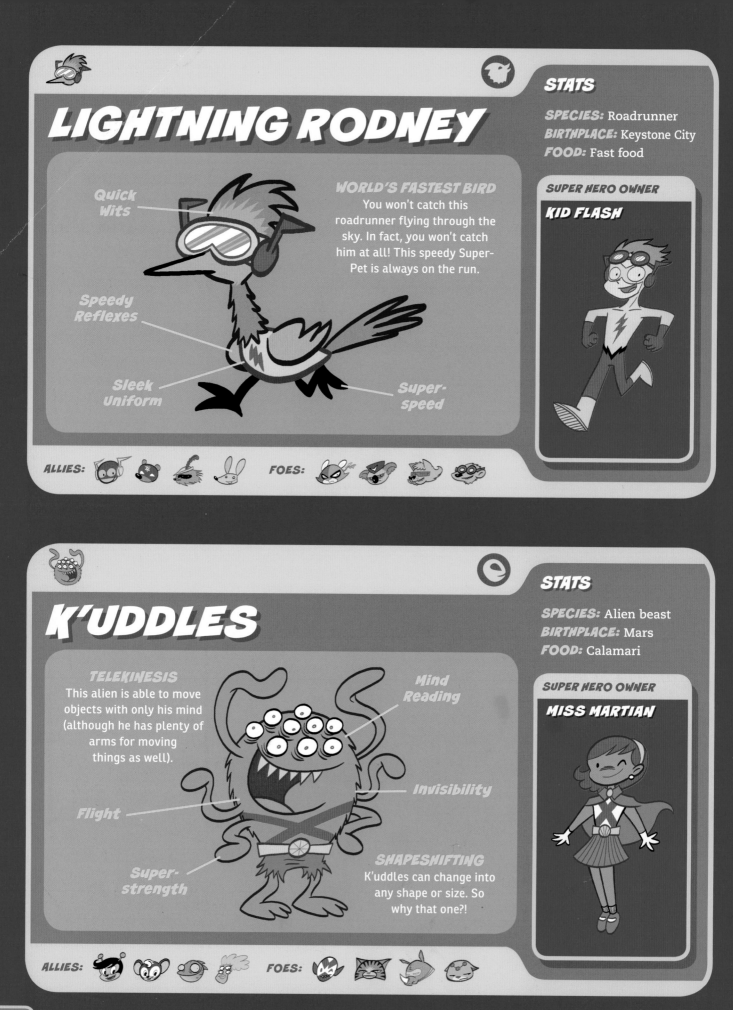

LIGHTNING RODNEY

STATS

SPECIES: Roadrunner
BIRTHPLACE: Keystone City
FOOD: Fast food

Quick Wits

Speedy Reflexes

Sleek Uniform

WORLD'S FASTEST BIRD
You won't catch this roadrunner flying through the sky. In fact, you won't catch him at all! This speedy Super-Pet is always on the run.

Super-speed

SUPER HERO OWNER

KID FLASH

ALLIES: **FOES:**

K'UDDLES

STATS

SPECIES: Alien beast
BIRTHPLACE: Mars
FOOD: Calamari

TELEKINESIS
This alien is able to move objects with only his mind (although he has plenty of arms for moving things as well).

Mind Reading

Flight

Invisibility

Super-strength

SHAPESHIFTING
K'uddles can change into any shape or size. So why that one?!

SUPER HERO OWNER

MISS MARTIAN

ALLIES: **FOES:**

GUACAMOLE

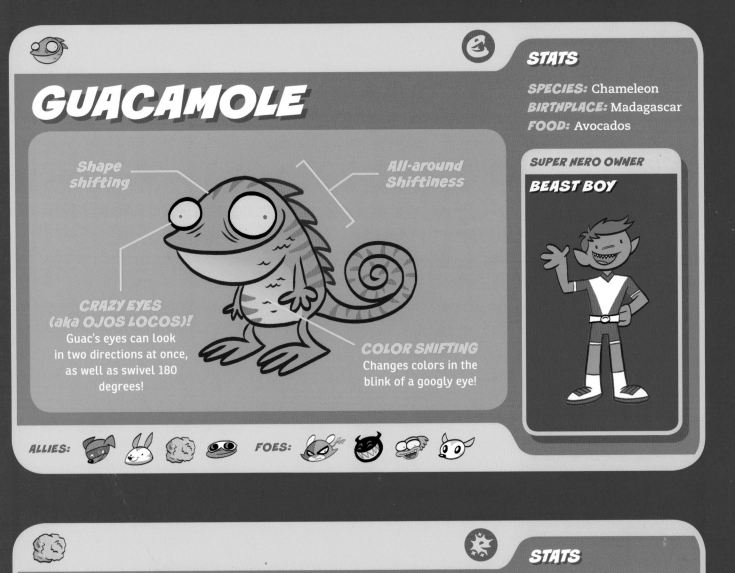

Shape shifting

All-around Shiftiness

CRAZY EYES (aka OJOS LOCOS)!
Guac's eyes can look in two directions at once, as well as swivel 180 degrees!

COLOR SHIFTING
Changes colors in the blink of a googly eye!

SUPER HERO OWNER
BEAST BOY

ALLIES: **FOES:**

THUD

STATS

SPECIES: Pet rock
BIRTHPLACE: Quarryville
FOOD: Rocky road ice cream

Control Over Rocks

Rock 'n' Roll Attitude

POWERFUL GEOMORPH
Thud is greater than granite! She's mightier than marble! When her owner, Terra, is stuck between a rock and a hard place, Thud can move the earth to save her.

Control Over Soil

SUPER HERO OWNER
TERRA

ALLIES: **FOES:**

SILKY

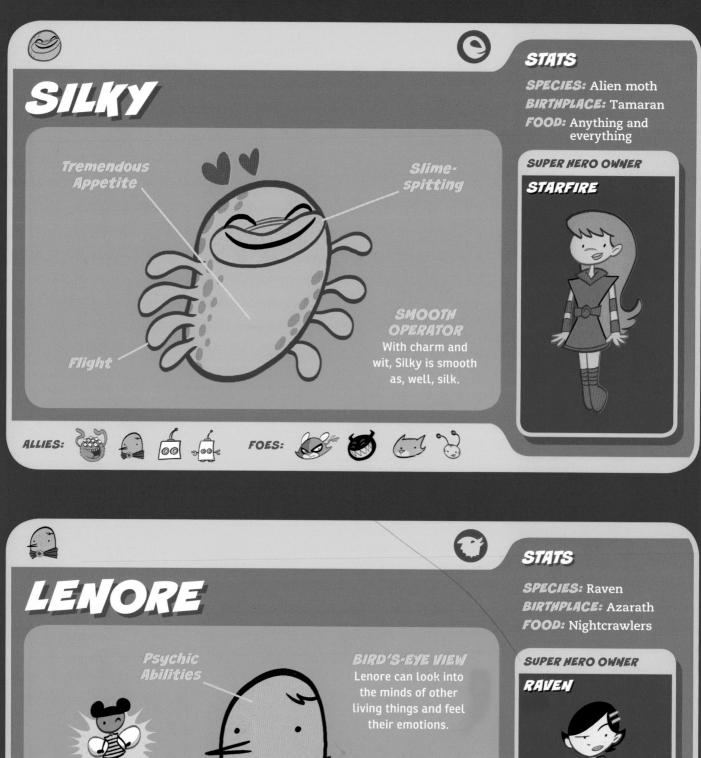

Tremendous Appetite

Slime-spitting

Flight

SMOOTH OPERATOR
With charm and wit, Silky is smooth as, well, silk.

STATS

SPECIES: Alien moth
BIRTHPLACE: Tamaran
FOOD: Anything and everything

SUPER HERO OWNER

STARFIRE

ALLIES:

FOES:

LENORE

Psychic Abilities

BIRD'S-EYE VIEW
Lenore can look into the minds of other living things and feel their emotions.

Flight

Healing Powers

BUMBLEBEE!
Although she's not a Super-Pet, this tiny teen hero can sting like a bee! But she'd never harm her best friend, Raven.

STATS

SPECIES: Raven
BIRTHPLACE: Azarath
FOOD: Nightcrawlers

SUPER HERO OWNER

RAVEN

ALLIES:

FOES:

PROTY

STATS

SPECIES: Llorn
BIRTHPLACE: Antares system
FOOD: Marshmallows

SECRET BIO:
After traveling to a planet in the Antares system, Chameleon Boy adopted Proty as his protoplasmic pet. This spineless specimen is much more than just a pile of goo. With unique shape-shifting abilities, Proty can transform into nearly any object in the universe. Or even multiple objects, making him a double—or sometimes even TRIPLE—threat!

FUN FACT!
Unlike most pets, Proty doesn't need air to breathe!

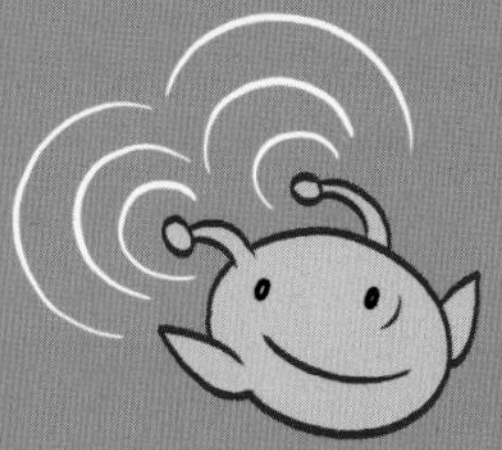

MIND-READER
Proteans from the Antares system, like Proty, communicate using only their minds. Proty can also read the minds of other beings.

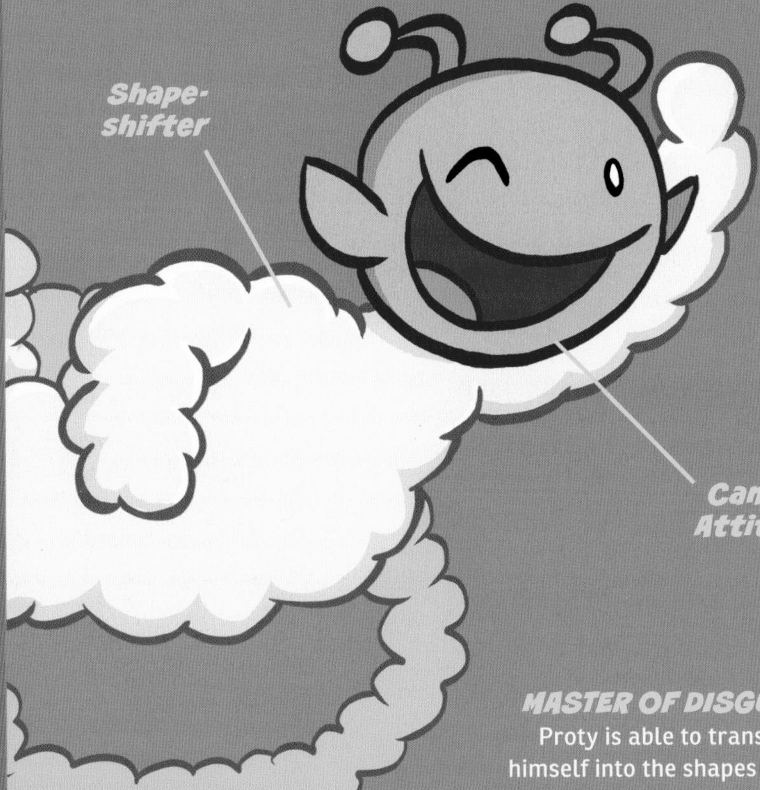

Shape-shifter
Can-do Attitude

MASTER OF DISGUISE!
Proty is able to transform himself into the shapes of other beings, including other DC Super-Pets!

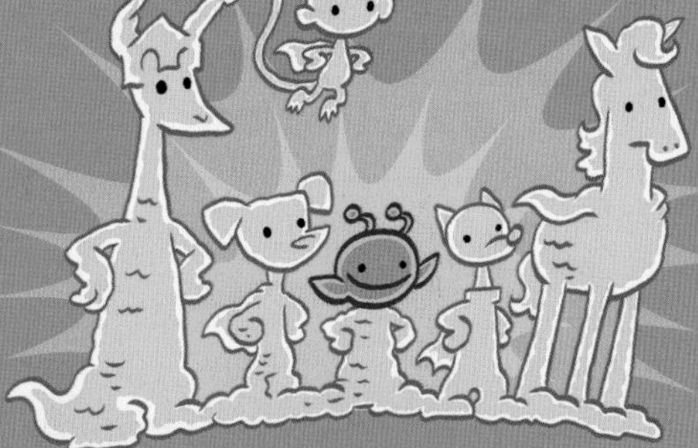

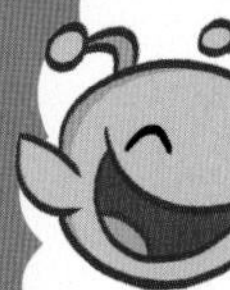

How do you organize a space party?
You plan-et!

SUPER HERO OWNER
CHAMELEON BOY

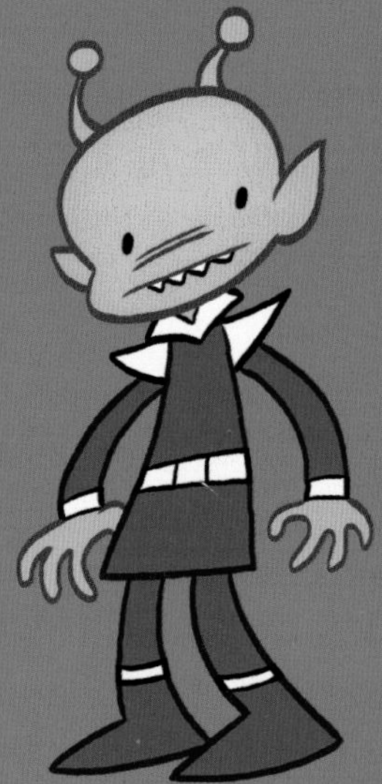

ALLIES: 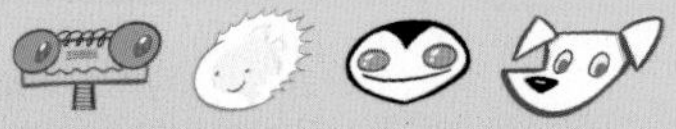
FOES: 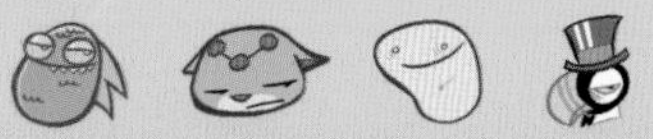

TARVOS

STATS

SPECIES: Alien
BIRTHPLACE: Titan
FOOD: Sashimi

TELEKINESIS
The ability to move physical objects using just her mind.

SEPTENARY LIMBS
Seven multi-purpose limbs allow Tarvos to move quickly and grapple with several villains at once!

Multiple Eyes

SUPER HERO OWNER

SATURN GIRL

ALLIES: **FOES:**

ZINKK

STATS

SPECIES: Alien
BIRTHPLACE: Braal
FOOD: Cosmic pizza

METALLIC UNIFORM
Zinkk uses the magnetic powers on his suit to help push or pull him through space.

GOGGLE EYES
Protects his eyes from ultra-cold or intense heat.

Magnetic Abilities

Extra Feet

SUPER HERO OWNER

COSMIC BOY

ALLIES: **FOES:**

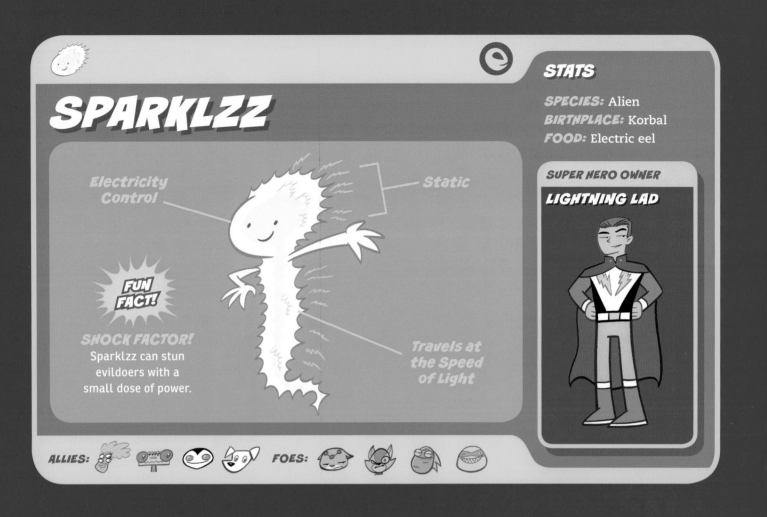

SPARKLZZ

Electricity Control

Static

FUN FACT!

SHOCK FACTOR!
Sparklzz can stun evildoers with a small dose of power.

Travels at the Speed of Light

SUPER HERO OWNER

LIGHTNING LAD

ALLIES: **FOES:**

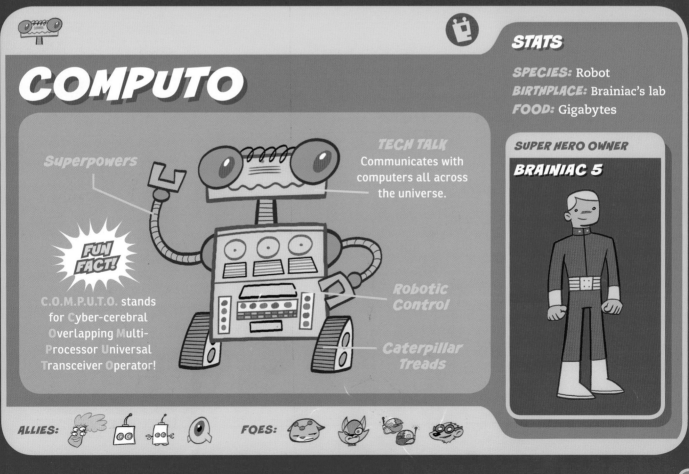

COMPUTO

STATS

SPECIES: Robot
BIRTHPLACE: Brainiac's lab
FOOD: Gigabytes

Superpowers

TECH TALK
Communicates with computers all across the universe.

FUN FACT!

C.O.M.P.U.T.O. stands for **C**yber-cerebral **O**verlapping **M**ulti-**P**rocessor **U**niversal **T**ransceiver **O**perator!

Robotic Control

Caterpillar Treads

SUPER HERO OWNER

BRAINIAC 5

ALLIES: **FOES:**

PRINCE TUFTAN

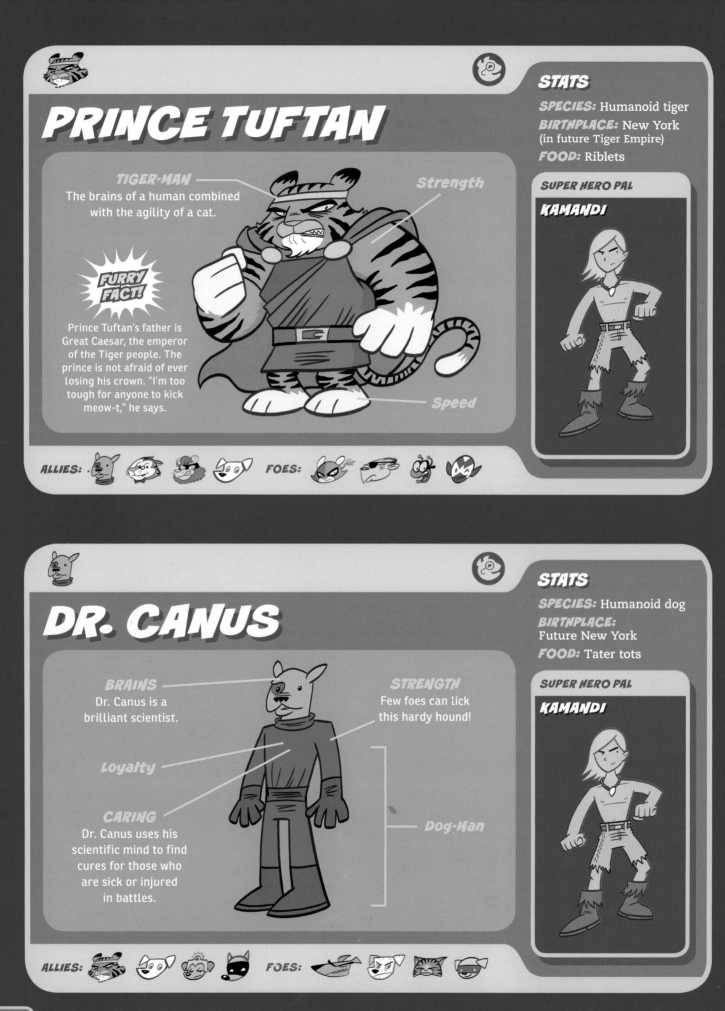

TIGER-MAN
The brains of a human combined with the agility of a cat.

FURRY FACT!
Prince Tuftan's father is Great Caesar, the emperor of the Tiger people. The prince is not afraid of ever losing his crown. "I'm too tough for anyone to kick meow-t," he says.

Strength

Speed

ALLIES: · **FOES:**

DR. CANUS

BRAINS
Dr. Canus is a brilliant scientist.

STRENGTH
Few foes can lick this hardy hound!

Loyalty

CARING
Dr. Canus uses his scientific mind to find cures for those who are sick or injured in battles.

Dog-Man

ALLIES: **FOES:**

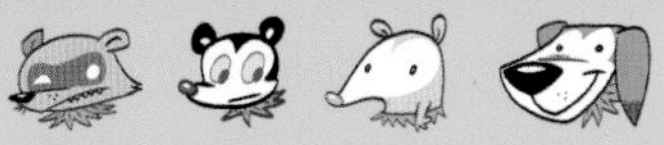

DOWN HOME CRITTER GANG

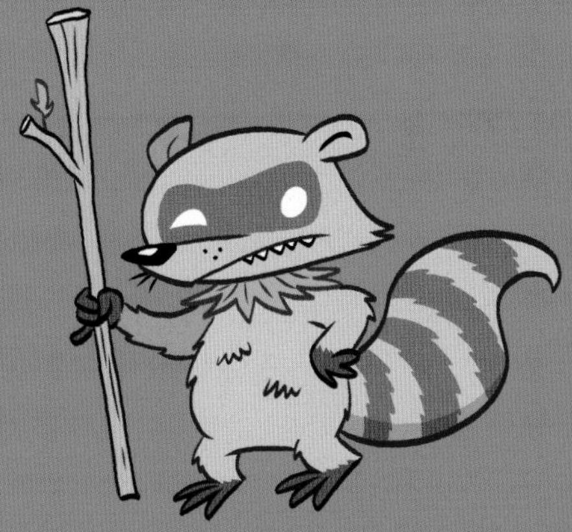

STARLENE
BREED: Raccoon
POWER: Stompin'
FOOD: Southern fried garbage

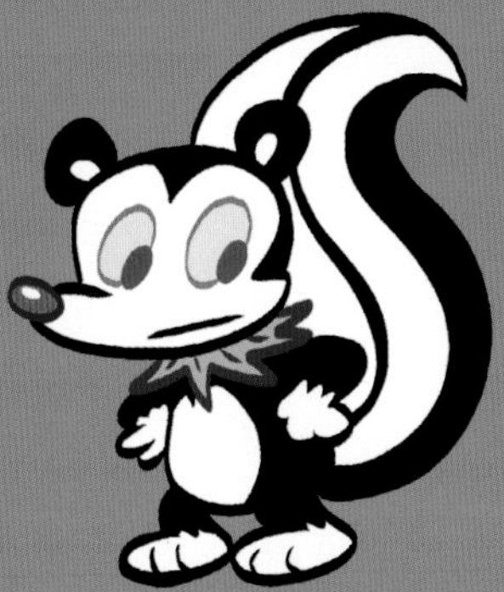

MOSSY
BREED: Skunk
POWER: Stinkin'
FOOD: Gumbo

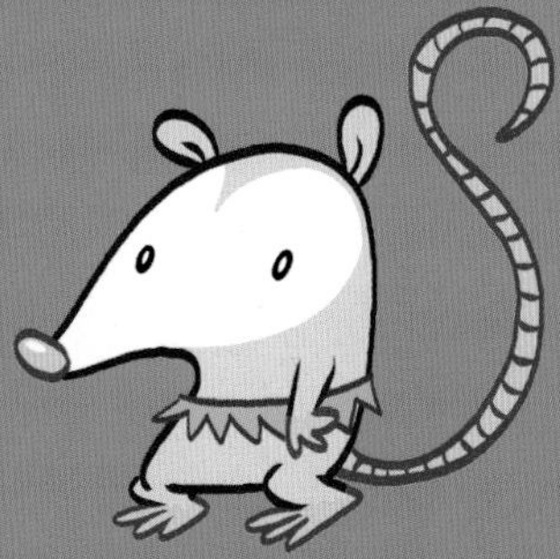

MERLE
BREED: Opossum
POWER: Swingin'
FOOD: Crawdads

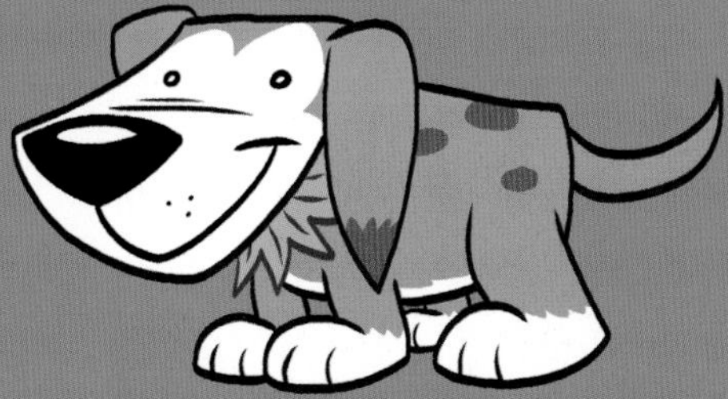

LOAFERS
BREED: Hound Dog
POWER: Loafin'
FOOD: Gator bones

STATS

SECRET BIO:
Members of the Down Home Critter Gang were born on a bayou. Like their super hero owner, Swamp Thing, they'll stop at nothing to protect their sacred swamps from Solomon Grundy's Undead Pet Club (*see page* 116) and other toxic terrors.

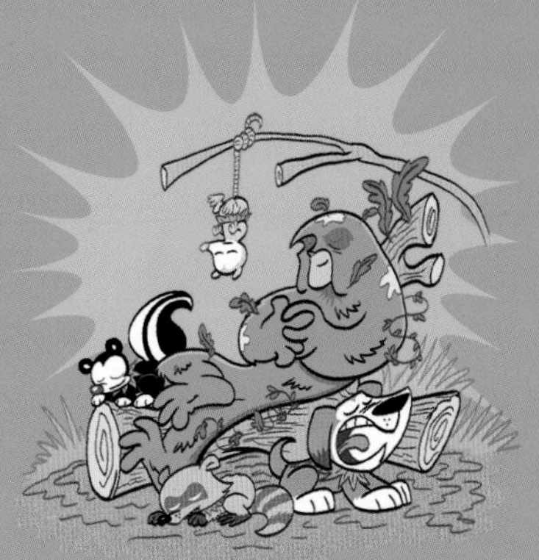

SUPER HERO OWNER

SWAMP THING

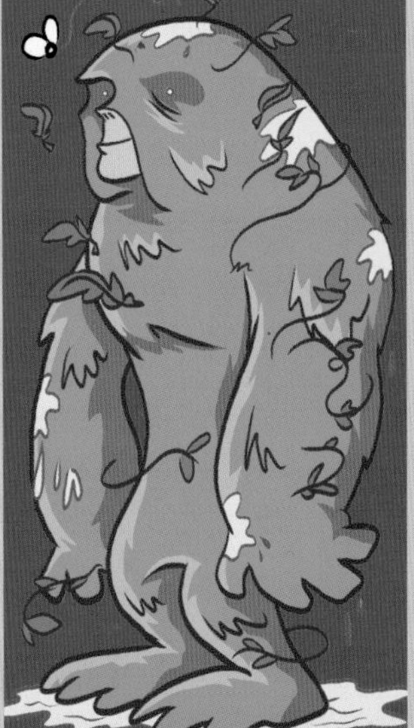

ALLIES: 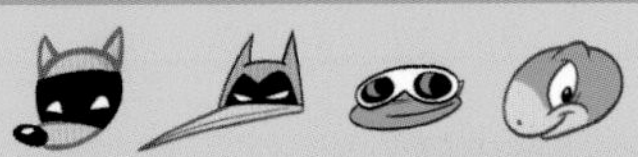 **FOES:** 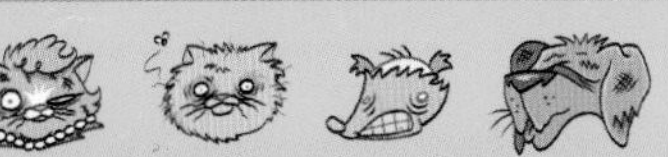

DAWG

STATS

SPECIES: Bulldog
BIRTHPLACE: Czarnia
FOOD: Bones

SECRET BIO:
This gruff growler was born to be wild! Looking for adventure, Dawg does not think of himself as a pet, but more as a partner. A handy hound to have on a hazardous hunt!

FURRY FACT!

Dawg sometimes goes by the alias "Mutt."

TRACKING SKILLS
While Dawg's nose can sniff out trouble, it doesn't mean that Dawg will *stay out* of trouble!

Thick Skull

Strength

Scrappy

Powerful Paws

THE SPACE HOG!
Dawg roams the universe with his owner, Lobo, the bounty hunter, on their Space Hog motorcycle.

SPACE DOLPHINS

SPECIES:
Alien dolphins
BIRTHPLACE:
Deep space
FOOD:
Starfish

SECRET BIO:
These clever creatures have extra-thick skin that protects them as they swim through the outer shores of space. They communicate with each other by telepathy.

SUPER HERO OWNER

LOBO

ALLIES:  **FOES:**

70

JEWELLION

STATS

SPECIES: Pegacorn
BIRTHPLACE: Gemworld
FOOD: Pearl onions

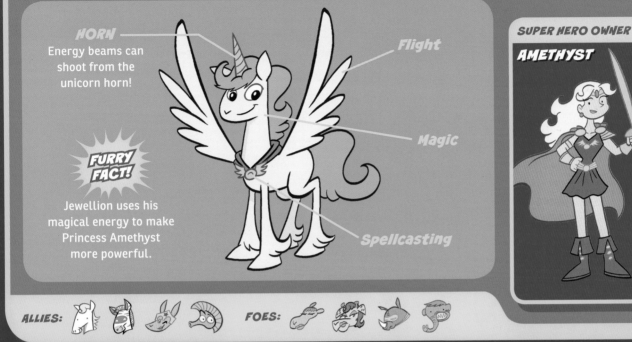

HORN
Energy beams can shoot from the unicorn horn!

Flight

Magic

FURRY FACT!
Jewellion uses his magical energy to make Princess Amethyst more powerful.

Spellcasting

SUPER HERO OWNER

AMETHYST

ALLIES: **FOES:**

VAPORS

STATS

SPECIES: Ghost pet
BIRTHPLACE: Himalayas
FOOD: Ghoulash

Teleportation

Invisibility

Ability to Heal

COURAGE
This fearless phantom is never spooked!

FURRY FACT!
Vapors is almost the perfect pet. He doesn't need to eat or sleep, and he never sheds!

Flight

SUPER HERO OWNER

DEADMAN

ALLIES: **FOES:**

SKITTERS

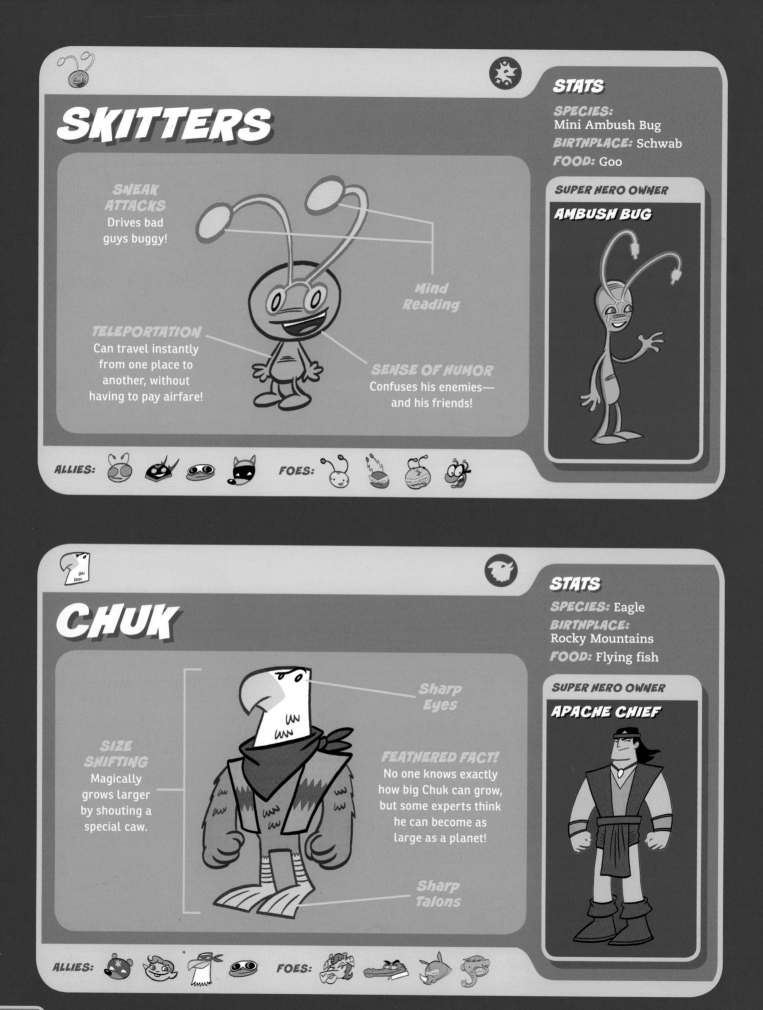

SNEAK ATTACKS
Drives bad guys buggy!

TELEPORTATION
Can travel instantly from one place to another, without having to pay airfare!

Mind Reading

SENSE OF HUMOR
Confuses his enemies— and his friends!

STATS
SPECIES: Mini Ambush Bug
BIRTHPLACE: Schwab
FOOD: Goo

SUPER HERO OWNER
AMBUSH BUG

ALLIES: **FOES:**

CHUK

SIZE SHIFTING
Magically grows larger by shouting a special caw.

Sharp Eyes

FEATHERED FACT!
No one knows exactly how big Chuk can grow, but some experts think he can become as large as a planet!

Sharp Talons

STATS
SPECIES: Eagle
BIRTHPLACE: Rocky Mountains
FOOD: Flying fish

SUPER HERO OWNER
APACHE CHIEF

ALLIES: **FOES:**

GLEEK

SPECIES: Space monkey
BIRTHPLACE: Exor
FOOD:
Banana cream pie

SECRET BIO:
On the planet Exor, Gleek starred in a traveling space circus. There he met the talented shape-shifters Zan and Jayna, known as the Wonder Twins. Together, the trio left the circus for new adventures, traveling through space and protecting the universe from evil.

FUN FACT!
Whenever Zan and Jayna cannot touch to activate their powers, Gleek can act as a "connector" by touching them both at the same time.

ELASTIC TAIL
This posterior appendage stretches to amazing lengths. It can bend, twist, become a bouncing coil, and turn into a lasso for roping bad guys.

Cheerful

Agile Climber

Sign Language

FRIENDLY SIXTH SENSE
Whenever the Wonder Twins change their shapes, Gleek can still recognize them.

THE WONDER TWINS
The Wonder Twins, Zan and Jayna, come from the planet Exor. Because of their amazing shape-shifting powers they were trapped as performers in the Space Circus. Once they escaped, they used their powers for good. Jayna can transform into any living creature from anywhere in the universe. Zan takes the shape of water, from a bridge of ice to a cloud of vapor. To transform, they must hold hands or bump fists together.

SUPER HERO OWNERS

THE WONDER TWINS, ZAN & JAYNA

ALLIES: **FOES:**

THE AMAZING ZOO CREW!

CAPTAIN CARROT (LEADER)

SPECIES: Rabbit
POWER: Super-strength; enhanced vision and hearing; stamina; leaping ability
FOOD: Carrots (obviously)

ALLEY-KAT-ABRA

SPECIES: Cat
POWER: Levitation; mystic force bolts; telepathy; teleportation; martial arts
FOOD: Wish bones

FASTBACK

SPECIES: Turtle
POWER: Super-speed
FOOD: Sweet corn

LITTLE CHEESE

SPECIES: Mouse
POWER: Shrinking ability
FOOD: Cheddar cheese

ALLIES:  **FOES:**

RUBBERDUCK

SPECIES: Duck
POWER: Stretchy
FOOD: Bathwater

YANKEE POODLE

SPECIES: Dog
POWER: Shoots stars from her right hand to repel objects; stripes with her left hand to attract objects
FOOD: Apple pie

PIG-IRON

SPECIES: Pig
POWER: Invulnerability; strength
FOOD: Mississippi mud cake

AMERICAN EAGLE

SPECIES: Eagle
POWER: Flight; strength
FOOD: Northern pike

STATS

BIO:
The alien invader Starro once blasted Earth with a powerful beam which began turning humans into animals! Superman used a meteor to repel the ray, but the space rock exploded and the fragments plunged into another dimension where animals ruled Earth. The critters struck by bits of the meteor gained superpowers. Captain Carrot of Gnu York was the first to discover his new abilities. He soon found others like him, and they banded together under his leadership as the Amazing Zoo Crew!

SUPER HERO PAL

SUPERMAN

HERO PETS SIZE CHART!

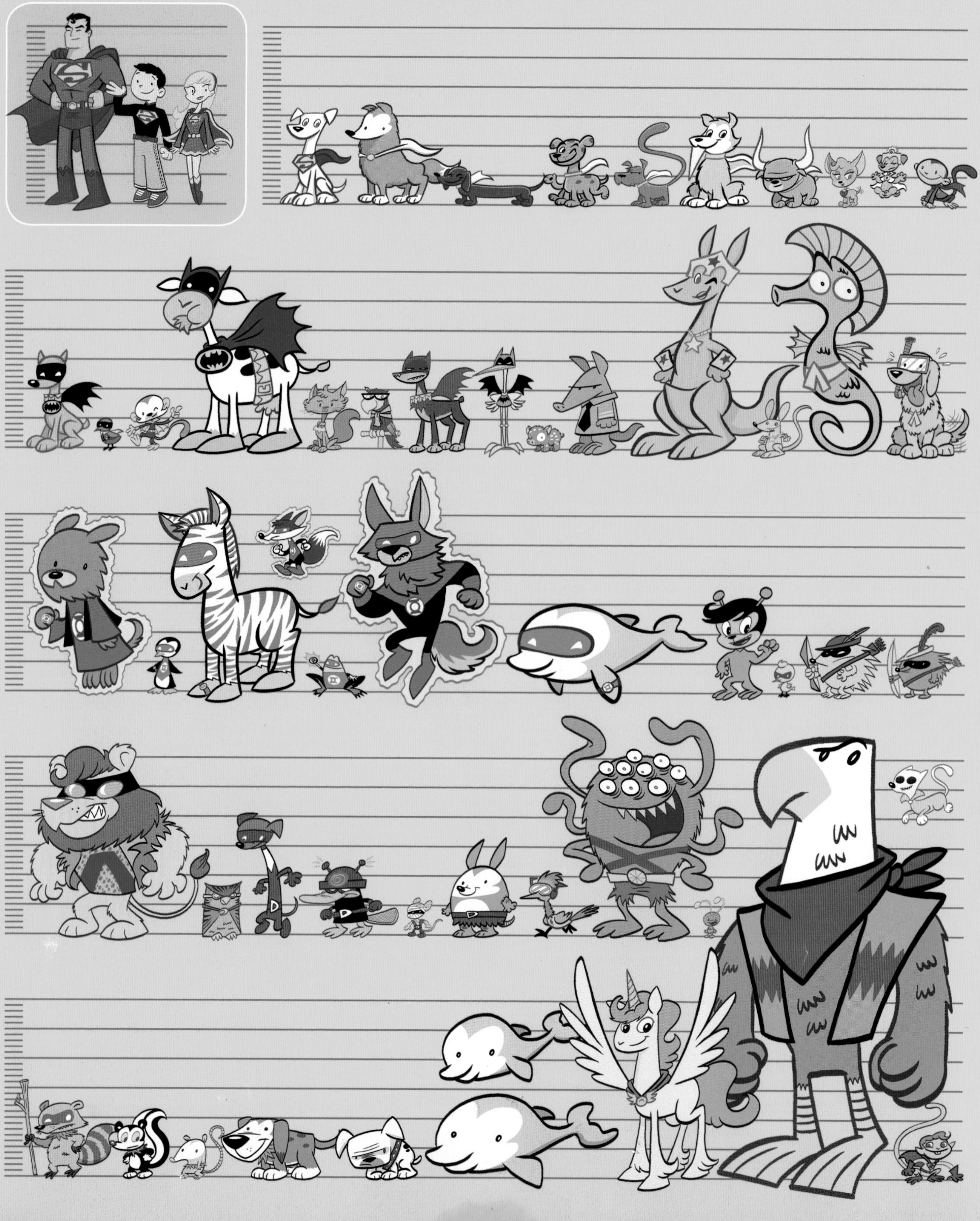

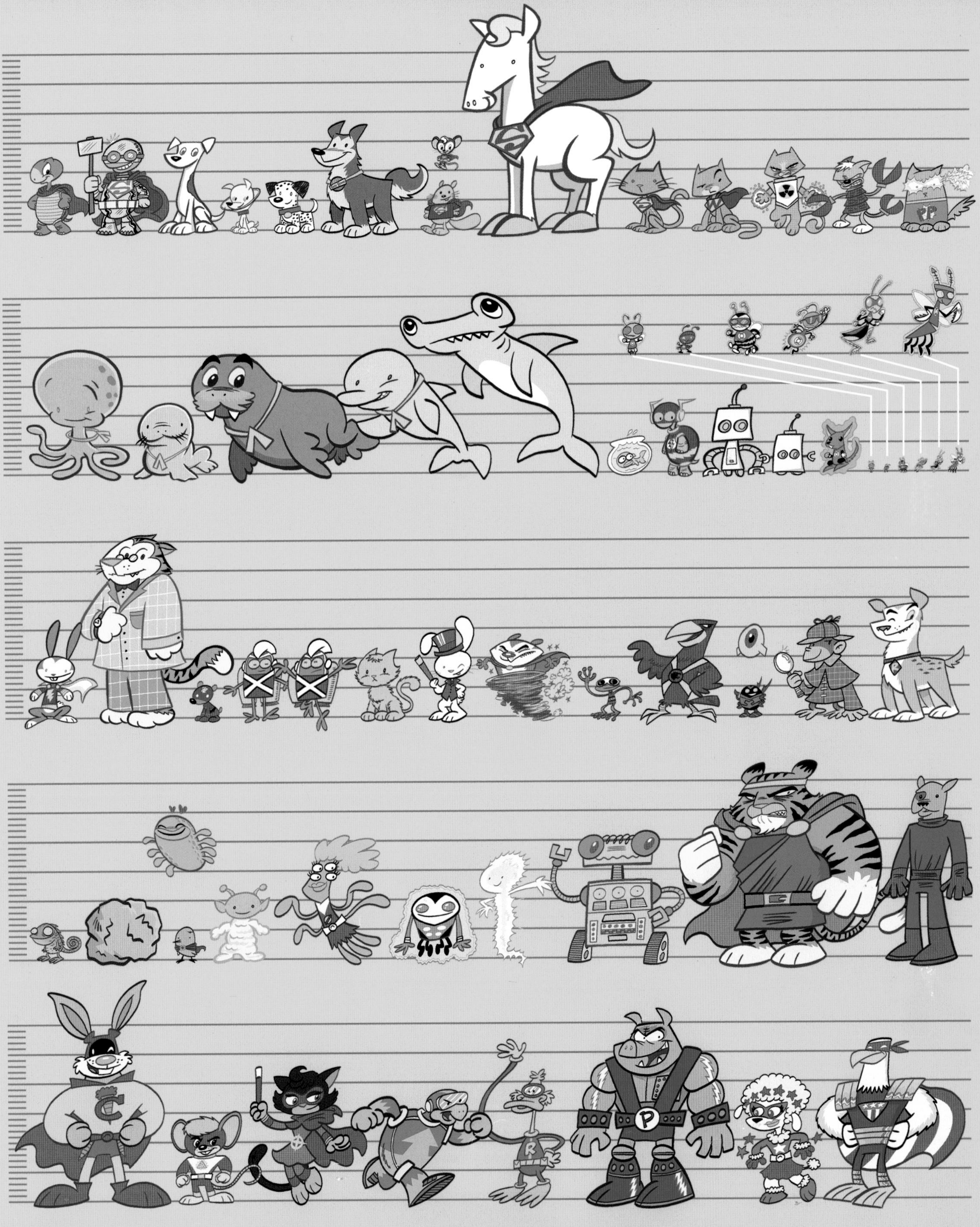

SECRET HISTORIES OF THE DC SUPER-PETS!

Robbie the Robot-Dog
(above) and Streak (right).

Krypto the Super-Dog appeared on
the cover of *Superboy* #109 in 1963.

Animals and DC Comics have been together since the company's very first comic book. Cowboy Jack Woods rode a white horse on the cover of *New Comics #1*, and Oswald the Rabbit hopped through two adventures inside that comic. Dogs, cats, monkeys, and other animals scampered through DC's comics for the next seven years, but it wasn't until 1944 that an official Super-Pet arrived in *Star Spangled Comics #29*. DC's first Super-Pet was made of metal! He was Robbie the Robot-Dog, the mechanical pet of Robotman. Four years later, another crime-fighting pooch said his first "Woof!" in *Green Lantern #30*. He was Streak the Wonder Dog, the bravest and smartest police dog of them all. Streak threw himself at gunmen, broke up criminal gangs, jumped off cliffs to save drowning children... and even testified in court! Streak became so popular that he even replaced Green Lantern on the cover of the super hero's own comic book!

Krypto the Super-Dog, the most famous DC Super-Pet of all, first flew into action in *Adventure Comics #210* in 1955, and he quickly became Superboy's closest companion. Krypto possessed the same superpowers as his Kryptonian master, and soon the Super-Dog became a charter member of the Legion of Super-Pets that included Streaky the Super-Cat (feline friend of Supergirl), Beppo the Super-Monkey, Comet the Super-Horse, and Proty II, a formless creature from the planet Antares. The Legion of Super-Pets was always ready to take a bite out of evildoers!

Since then, a mighty menagerie of heroic and criminal animals, birds, and fishes have joined the action. No longer just sidekicks to their super hero companions or scheming super-villains, the DC Super-Pets are now superstars in the DC Universe!

In *Batman* #97 (1956), Ace the Bat-Hound helped the Dynamic Duo solve a case.

Destructo first appeared in *Superboy* #92 in 1961.

The "All Pet Club Issue!" of *Tiny Titans* #12, published in 2009.

The Terrific Whatzit, as depicted in *Funny Stuff* #1 (1944).

The origin of Comet was revealed in *Action Comics* #293 in 1962.

Storm appeared on the cover of *Aquaman* #12 in 1963.

In 1942, Wonder Woman rode a kanga on the cover of *Sensation Comics* #6.

VILLAIN PETS!

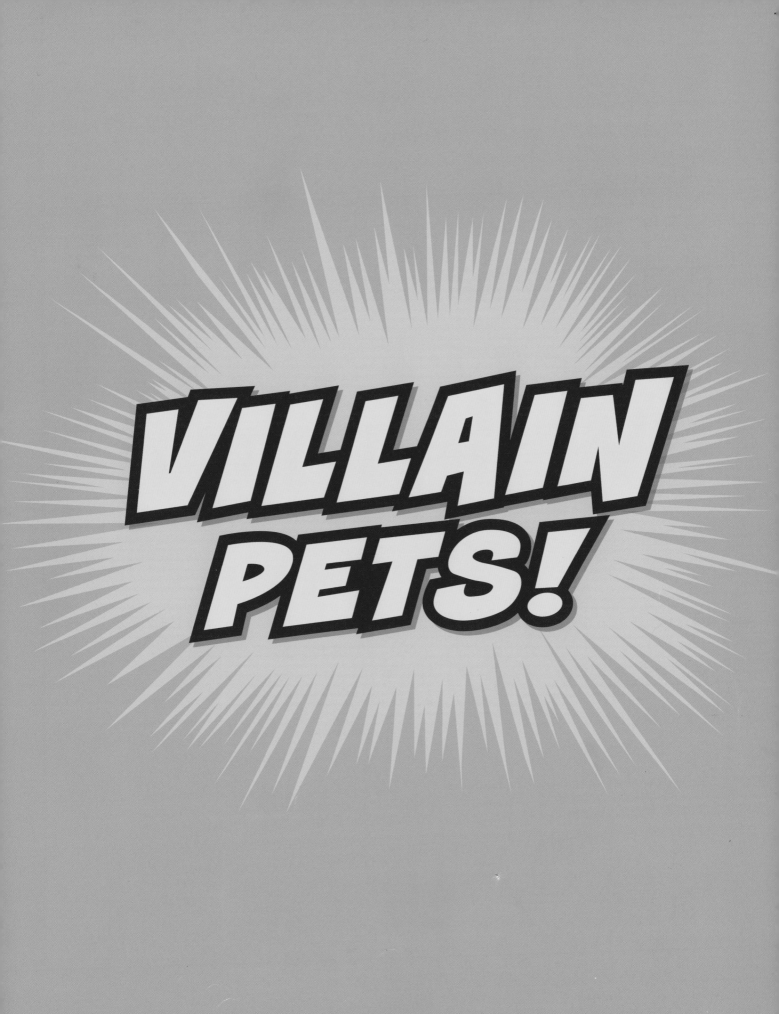

BIZARRO KRYPTO

FLAME BREATH!
Bizarro Krypto's superpowers are the opposite of Krypto the Super-Dog's powers. Instead of Freeze Breath, Bizarro Krypto breathes super-hot FLAMES!

Ice Vision

Super-hearing

Super-smell

Flight

Backward S-shield

Super-speed

SECRET BIO:
When Krypto the Super-Dog crashed on Htrae, the Bizarros created his evil twin and named him Bizarro Krypto. The Bizarro Dog is the complete opposite of his Kryptonian counterpart, but he's just as powerful. On Htrae, this backward bowwow gets his superpowers from the planet's blue sun.

WEAKNESS:
Blue Kryptonite (*see page 22*)

SUPER-VILLAIN OWNER

BIZARRO

FURRY FACTS!

AQUA-OH'S!
Bizarro Krypto's favorite Earth cereal is Aqua-Oh's!

Krypto-MIGHT!
Bizarro Krypto is not hurt by green Kryptonite.

SCAREDY-DOG?
On the backward planet Htrae, dogs are afraids of cats!

ALLIES: FOES:

HTRAE, THE BACKWARD EARTH

The Bizarro planet of Htrae is the exact opposite of Earth. Besides being square, Htrae's sun is blue. Also, dogs rule this backward planet, not humans! Weird, huh?

HTRAE

EARTH

Krypto isn't the only Super-Pet with a backward double. Check out these other Bizarro Pets!

BIZARRO STREAKY
POWER: Flame Breath
FOOD: Toast and coffee

BIZARRO BEPPO
POWER: Seriousness
FOOD: Banana-covered chocolates

BIZARRO TURTLE
POWER: Slowness
FOOD: Bizarro turtle treats

BIZARRO FUZZY
POWER: Arctic Vision
FOOD: Blue yogurt

BIZARRO COMET
POWER: Horsing around
FOOD: Monster cookies

IGNATIUS

SPECIES: Iguana
BIRTHPLACE: Metropolis
FOOD: Leafy greens

SECRET BIO:
Ignatius is the cool, calculating pet of Superman's archenemy, Lex Luthor. He may be cold-blooded, but this vile reptile is a real hot-head. Like his owner, he'll stop at nothing to take down Krypto the Super-Dog and his Kryptonian counterparts. With genius-level intelligence and a mastery of technology, Ignatius is a worthy opponent to any super hero.

COLD-BLOODED!
Ignatius is a cold-blooded crook. And that's no joke! Like all reptiles, this iguana needs the rays of Earth's yellow sun to warm his cool body.

Wicked Smart

KRYPTONITE
This radioactive rock is one of Ignatius' most powerful weapons.

HOPS
Leaping lizard!

Strong Tail

What does a lizard vampire say before he bites you?

"Iguana suck your blood!"

THE LEGION OF VILLAIN PETS!
Ignatius often considers himself the leader of the Legion of Villain Pets, which includes other evil animals!

SUPER-VILLAIN OWNER

LEX LUTHOR

ALLIES: **FOES:**

DESTRUCTO

STATS

SPECIES: Dog
BIRTHPLACE: Metropolis
FOOD: Kibble

Heat & X-ray Vision

Super-smell

Super-hearing

Skull & Crossbones Cape

Flight

Super-speed

FURRY FACT!

When Lex Luthor's pet dog Wolf stepped in front of his master's experimental ray gun, he gained superpowers! Destructo has the same powers as Krypto (*see page* 10).

SUPER-VILLAIN OWNER

LEX LUTHOR

ALLIES: **FOES:**

TITANO

STATS

SPECIES: Super-Ape
BIRTHPLACE: Metropolis
FOOD: Bananas

KRYPTONITE VISION
Blasts Kryptonite beams from his eyes!

Super-strength

Amazing Growth

FURRY FACT!

Titano was once just an average-sized ape.

SUPER-VILLAIN OWNER

LEX LUTHOR

ALLIES: **FOES:**

OMEGAN

SPECIES: Parademon
BIRTHPLACE: Apokolips
FOOD: Seared steak

SECRET BIO:
Omegan's owner, Darkseid, is immortal, meaning he'll live forever. Sounds great, right? But Darkseid has found that eternal life can get kind of boring sometimes. So, he created Omegan to keep him company—and carry out evil tasks that he can't trust his other Parademons with.

MOTHER BOX!
Omegan possesses a device called a Mother Box, which takes care of him and has the power to heal him when he's sick.

OMEGAN BEAMS
Like Darkseid, Omegan can fire Omega Beams from his eyes. The powerful blasts can bend around objects, ensuring they'll hit their mark!

Razor-sharp Claws

Flight

Agility

FUN FACT!
Like his master, Omegan can open Boom Tubes—dimensional tears which allow him to travel instantly from one place to another.

SUPER-VILLAIN OWNER

DARKSEID

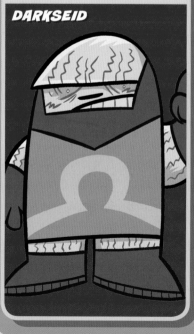

ALLIES: **FOES:**

PHANTY-CATS

GENERAL MANX

BREED: Abyssinian
BIRTHPLACE: Krypton
FOOD: Tuna pot pie

NIZZ

BREED: Sphynx
BIRTHPLACE: Krypton
FOOD: Duck

FER-EL

BREED: Orange tabby
BIRTHPLACE: Krypton
FOOD: Star junk

PHANTOM ZONE CRIMINALS

SUPER-VILLAIN OWNER
GENERAL ZOD

SUPER-VILLAIN OWNER
URSA

SUPER-VILLAIN OWNER
NON

STATS

SECRET BIO:
For years, these feline felons terrorized the galaxy by robbing planets—until the Space Canine Patrol Agents (*see page* 12), led by Krypto (*see page 10*), caught the cats and trapped them in the Phantom Zone. The interdimensional prison for superpowered criminals held the felines for a while, but eventually General Manx found a way out.

INVISIBILITY!
After escaping the Phantom Zone, the Phanty-Cats created a potion that turned them invisible, making them formidable foes.

The Phanty-Cats' worst nightmare is shed fur, which reveals their true form, even when invisible.

ALLIES: **FOES:**

BRAINICAT

Wicked Smart

CAT NAPPING
Traveling light years through space is a tiring task!

Cold-hearted

Super-strength

Super-strong Tail

STATS

SPECIES: Alien cat
BIRTHPLACE: Colu
FOOD: Catnip cake

SECRET BIO:
As a lonely scientist on the planet Colu, Brainiac decided to create the ultimate feline friend—Brainicat! Like his evil master, this cold-blooded kitty is big on brains and small on heart.

SHRINKING CITIES!
Using an incredible shrinking ray, Brainicat collects entire cities inside milk bottles.

BRAINICAT SKULL SHIP

Brainicat's specially designed Skull Ship allows the killer kitty to travel throughout the universe. No steering wheel is required for this sinister spacecraft. Brainicat controls the ship with his mind! Its many weapons include red-sun torpedoes, capable of making Krypto tuck tail and run.

SUPER-VILLAIN OWNER

BRAINIAC

ALLIES:

FOES:

MECHANIKAT

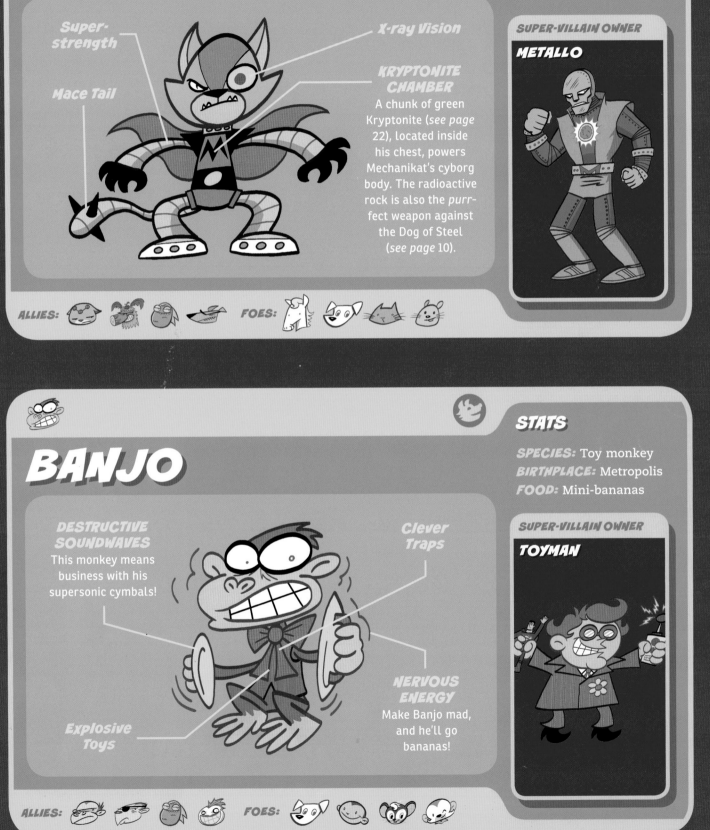

Super-strength

Mace Tail

X-ray Vision

KRYPTONITE CHAMBER
A chunk of green Kryptonite (*see page 22*), located inside his chest, powers Mechanikat's cyborg body. The radioactive rock is also the *purr-fect* weapon against the Dog of Steel (*see page 10*).

(see page 22)
(see page 10)

STATS

SPECIES: Cyborg cat
BIRTHPLACE: Metropolis
FOOD: Computer chips

SUPER-VILLAIN OWNER
METALLO

ALLIES: FOES:

BANJO

DESTRUCTIVE SOUNDWAVES
This monkey means business with his supersonic cymbals!

Clever Traps

NERVOUS ENERGY
Make Banjo mad, and he'll go bananas!

Explosive Toys

STATS

SPECIES: Toy monkey
BIRTHPLACE: Metropolis
FOOD: Mini-bananas

SUPER-VILLAIN OWNER
TOYMAN

ALLIES: FOES:

CRACKERS

Wicked Grin

Sharp Hearing

Razor-sharp Teeth

Evil Heart

Funny Bone

TRICKS WITH TREATS!
Crackers can't "sit" to save his life, but he excels at tripping up foes using clever tricks!

STATS

SPECIES: Laughing hyena

BIRTHPLACE: Arkham Asylum, Gotham City

FOOD: Saltines

SECRET BIO:
The Joker doesn't always get along with his sidekick, Harley Quinn, but he sure did love the laughing hyena she got him—after all, the crazy hyena never stops cackling!

FURRY FACT!
Crackers got his name because the Joker taught his pup to eat all of Harley's saltines.

SUPER-VILLAIN OWNER

THE JOKER

JOKER FISH

SPECIES: Clown fish

BIRTHPLACE: Gotham City Harbor

FOOD: Plankton

SECRET BIO:
When Harley gave the Joker a clown fish for his birthday, the Clown Prince of Crime was so pleased that he invited all of his felonious friends for a toxic pool party.

ALLIES: **FOES:**

GIGGLES

SPECIES: Laughing hyena

BIRTHPLACE: Arkham Asylum, Gotham City

FOOD: Laughing gas

SECRET BIO:
While Giggles is Crackers' twin brother, the two have very little in common. Crackers loves to laugh while Giggles prefers to scowl. Giggles is loyal to Harley while Crackers only obeys the Joker. But both brothers have one thing in common: harassing super hero pets!

FURRY FACT!
Giggles once tried to eat a Joker Fish, but spat it out after discovering it tasted funny.

Sharp Hearing

Wicked Grin

Razor-sharp Teeth

Evil Heart

Funny Bone

SUPER-VILLAIN OWNER
HARLEY QUINN

DECEPTIVE NATURE
Like the Joker, Giggles and Crackers love to pull pranks!

ALLIES: **FOES:**

BAD NEWS BIRDS

ICE DICE!
One toss of Artie's high-tech dice means bad luck for any foe caught in their icy blast!

ARTIE PUFFIN (LEADER)
SPECIES: Puffin
POWERS: Cold and calculating
FOOD: Sardines

WADDLES
SPECIES: Penguin
POWER: Sharp beak
FOOD: Herring

GRIFF
SPECIES: Vulture
POWER: Chilly heart
FOOD: Carrion

STATS

SECRET BIO:
These bad birds might not all have feathers, but they definitely flock together whenever the Penguin has some dirty deeds in mind. Artie the Puffin is the leader of their fowl little gang, but Waddles and Griff don't always fly in formation.

THE PENGUIN SUB
The Penguin's underwater craft is modeled after a swimming penguin and operated by his gang, the Bad New Birds.

SUPER-VILLAIN OWNER
THE PENGUIN

ALLIES: **FOES:**

ROZZ

STATS

SPECIES: Siamese cat
BIRTHPLACE: Gotham City
FOOD: Milk

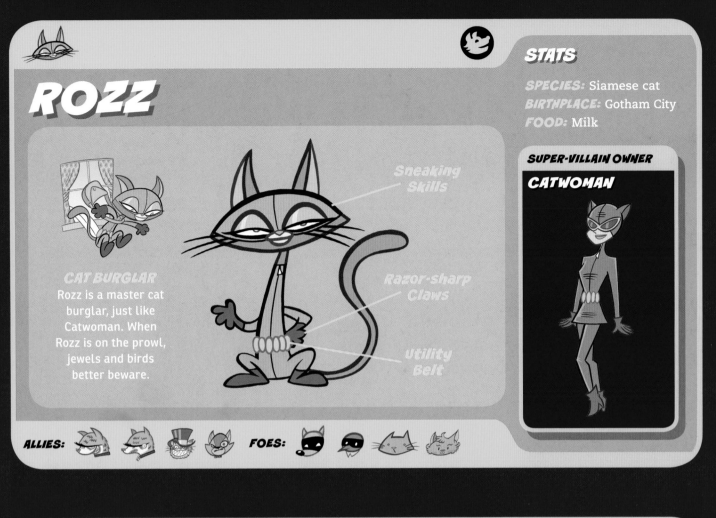

Sneaking Skills

Razor-sharp Claws

Utility Belt

CAT BURGLAR

Rozz is a master cat burglar, just like Catwoman. When Rozz is on the prowl, jewels and birds better beware.

SUPER-VILLAIN OWNER

CATWOMAN

ALLIES:  **FOES:**

OSITO

STATS

SPECIES: Bear cub
BIRTHPLACE: Santa Prisca
FOOD: Honeycomb

Venomous Temper

LUCHADOR MASK

Osito's mask is similar to the ones Mexican wrestlers, or *luchadores*, wear.

Enhanced Strength

Powerful Paws

FURRY FACT!

Osito's name means "little bear" in Spanish, his native language. Bane named his bear buddy after a stuffed animal he had as a child.

SUPER-VILLAIN OWNER

BANE

ALLIES: **FOES:**

CROWARD

Eerie Mask

Creepy Caw

SCARY DUST
Any foe who inhales Croward's Scary Dust is sure to cower in fear.

THE SCAREDY CROWS!
This murder of crows loves to frighten its foes, making them the most foul flock on the block.

STATS
SPECIES: Crow
BIRTHPLACE: Arkham Asylum, Gotham City
FOOD: Candy corn

SUPER-VILLAIN OWNER
SCARECROW

ALLIES: **FOES:**

DOGWOOD

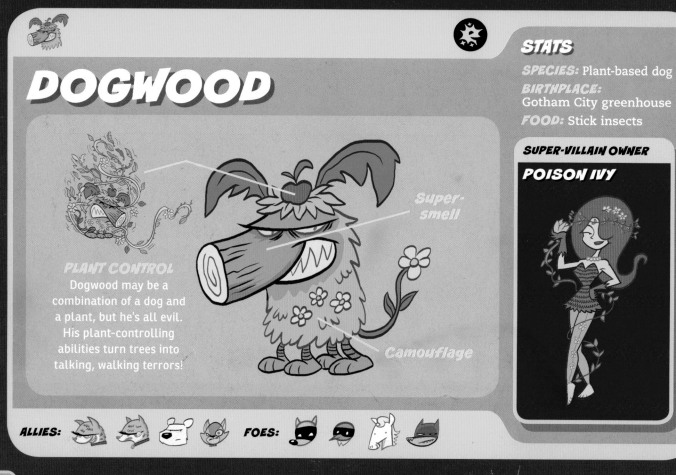

Super-smell

PLANT CONTROL
Dogwood may be a combination of a dog and a plant, but he's all evil. His plant-controlling abilities turn trees into talking, walking terrors!

Camouflage

STATS
SPECIES: Plant-based dog
BIRTHPLACE: Gotham City greenhouse
FOOD: Stick insects

SUPER-VILLAIN OWNER
POISON IVY

ALLIES: **FOES:**

OTTO

SUPER-VILLAIN OWNER

THE RIDDLER

MASTER HUNTER
Whether he's hunting for answers to riddles or trying to track down an enemy, this bird of prey is sure to find what he's looking for.

Wise Mind

Sharp Beak

Sharp Talons

ALLIES: **FOES:**

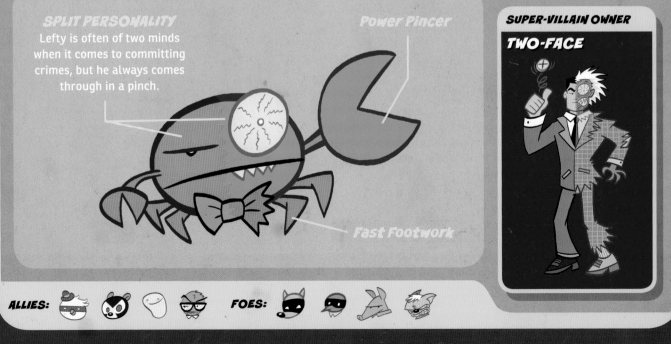

LEFTY

STATS

SPECIES: Fiddler crab
BIRTHPLACE: Gotham City Harbor
FOOD: Banana splits

SUPER-VILLAIN OWNER

TWO-FACE

SPLIT PERSONALITY
Lefty is often of two minds when it comes to committing crimes, but he always comes through in a pinch.

Power Pincer

Fast Footwork

ALLIES: **FOES:**

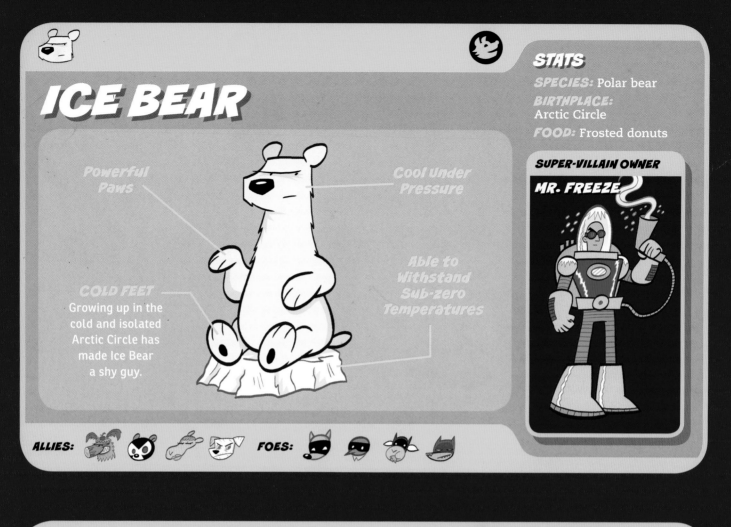

ICE BEAR

Powerful Paws

Cool Under Pressure

COLD FEET
Growing up in the cold and isolated Arctic Circle has made Ice Bear a shy guy.

Able to Withstand Sub-zero Temperatures

STATS
SPECIES: Polar bear
BIRTHPLACE: Arctic Circle
FOOD: Frosted donuts

SUPER-VILLAIN OWNER
MR. FREEZE

ALLIES: **FOES:**

SĀNDY

Quick Wits

STAMINA
Sāndy has a sturdy back and can store fat in her hump, making her an excellent form of desert transportation for her owner.

FURRY FACT!

IMMORTALITY
Sāndy drinks from the Lazarus Pits. She stores the magical water in her hump, keeping her happy and healthy.

Swift Kicks

STATS
SPECIES: Camel
BIRTHPLACE: Horn of Africa
FOOD: Sandwiches

SUPER-VILLAIN OWNER
RĀ'S AL GHŪL

ALLIES: **FOES:**

96

MAD CATTER

Hypnotizing Hat

Mind Control

Evil Grin

HAT COLLECTOR
Like his owner, Mad Catter wears many hats.

SUPER-VILLAIN OWNER
MAD HATTER

ALLIES: **FOES:**

GOOP

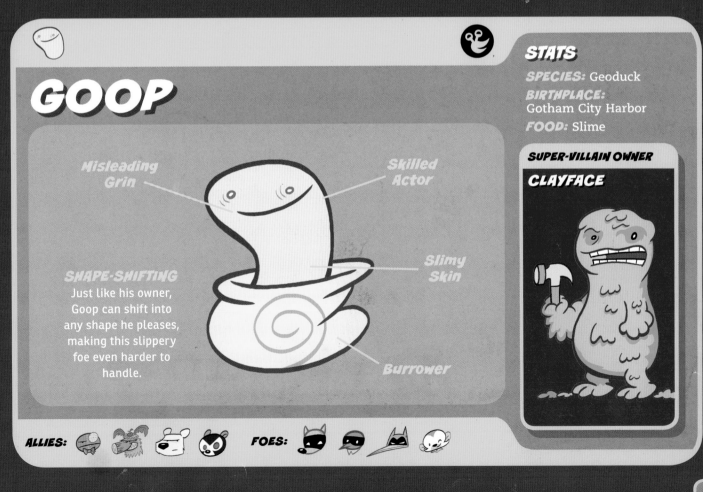

STATS

SPECIES: Geoduck
BIRTHPLACE: Gotham City Harbor
FOOD: Slime

Misleading Grin

Skilled Actor

Slimy Skin

Burrower

SHAPE-SHIFTING
Just like his owner, Goop can shift into any shape he pleases, making this slippery foe even harder to handle.

SUPER-VILLAIN OWNER
CLAYFACE

ALLIES: **FOES:**

ANNA CONDA

STATS

SPECIES: Giant anaconda
BIRTHPLACE: South America
FOOD: Frog's legs

Mouthy

Good Swimmer

FASHION SENSE
This snake loves to accesssssorize.

FUN FACT!

Anna Conda has a dangerous mouth, but she doesn't like to chew the fat. In fact, she doesn't chew at all. She can open her jaws wide and swallow her prey whole.

SUPER-VILLAIN PARTNER

KROC

ALLIES:  **FOES:**

DR. SPIDER

STATS

SPECIES: Tarantula
BIRTHPLACE: Brazil
FOOD: Sticky buns

Brilliant Evil Mind

MULTI-TASKING
With eight hairy limbs, this scientist can work on several computers, search the web, and deploy evil weapons all at the same time, including his no-good gas machine.

Enhanced Eyesight

Pocket Protector

SUPER-VILLAIN PARTNER

KROC

ALLIES: **FOES:**

ALLIES OR FOES?

Like their owners, these mischievous animals give the Super-Pets a hard time. But are they friends or foes?

DRIBODOD

POWER DERBY — Protects head against weird weather changes while transporting between dimensions.

Sense of Humor

FUN FACT!

Dribodod accompanies his impish owner, Mr. Mxyzptlk, when he travels to Earth in order to prank Superman. The fun-loving fowl can only be defeated if he is tricked into saying his name backward!

STATS

SPECIES: Flightless bird
BIRTHPLACE: Fifth Dimension
FOOD: *Dees* and *smrow*

OWNER
MR. MXYZPTLK

ALLIES? **FOES?**

ACE-MITE

Wealth of Knowledge on Ace

Flight

Magical Sense of Smell

LOYALTY
Just as his owner is Batman's biggest fan, Ace-Mite idolizes Ace the Bat-Hound (*see page 24*).

STATS

SPECIES: Toy terrier
BIRTHPLACE: Fifth Dimension
FOOD: Mini corn dogs

OWNER
BAT-MITE

ALLIES? **FOES?**

CHAUNCEY

RECORD-BREAKING SPEED

The fastest land animal on Earth, Chauncey can reach 100 miles an hour in only five seconds!

Night Vision

Razor-sharp Claws

AGILITY

Chauncey can jump, bounce, twist, and turn with, uh, catlike quickness.

FAST FACT!

His rival is Jumpa, Wonder Woman's kanga companion. Chauncey can always beat the leaper in an all-out race, but he just can't out-jump Jumpa.

Why can't you play cards in the jungle?
There are too many cheetahs!

SECRET BIO:
Chauncey was born and grew up on the savannahs of southern central Africa. But he was captured and imprisoned in a Washington, D.C. zoo. It was there that he snagged the attention of his owner Cheetah, who believed all felines should be free. Chauncey showed his gratitude by helping out Cheetah on her criminal capers, avenging himself against humankind who tricked and trapped him.

SUPER-VILLAIN OWNER

CHEETAH

ALLIES: **FOES:**

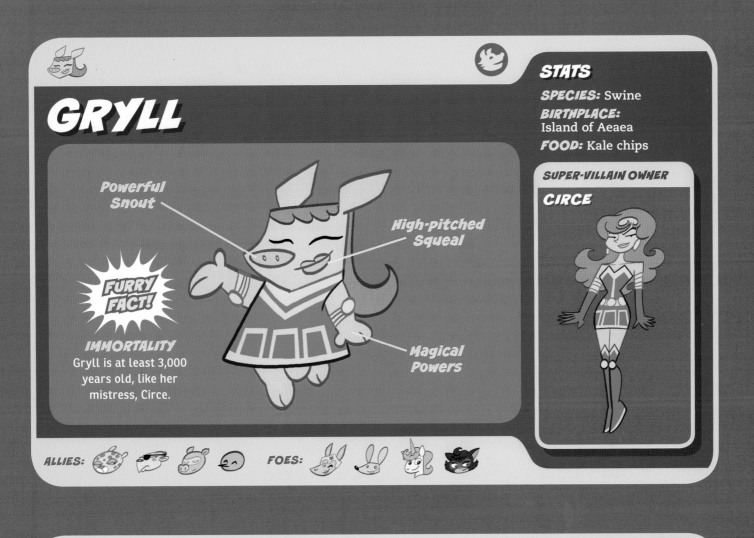

GRYLL

Powerful Snout

High-pitched Squeal

FURRY FACT!

IMMORTALITY
Gryll is at least 3,000 years old, like her mistress, Circe.

Magical Powers

SUPER-VILLAIN OWNER
CIRCE

ALLIES: **FOES:**

COMO

Cool Eye Patch

Telepathy

MENTAL SHIELD
Creates a protective force field around himself using only his brainpower.

Mind Control

SUPER-VILLAIN PAL
GORILLA GRODD

ALLIES: **FOES:**

MISTY

SPECIES: Stingray
BIRTHPLACE: Deep ocean
FOOD: Cold plate specials

Diving and Swimming

CAMOUFLAGE
Misty can flatten herself on the seafloor to hide from her enemies, like anemones.

Poisonous Tail

SNEEZERS

SPECIES: Stingray
BIRTHPLACE: Outside Atlantis
FOOD: Cough drops

Amazing Sense of Smell

SEAMANSHIP
Navigates through the deepest regions of the seven seas.

DEADLY TAIL
He can sting his foes with venom in his tricky tail.

STATS

SECRET BIO:
These two saltwater scoundrels follow their master, the oceanic evildoer Black Manta, on his many missions to trawl for treasure. They also help him hunt down Aquaman, King of Atlantis. The bad-guy buddies only trust each other. And with their speed, their awesome teamwork, and their dangerous tails, they make a deadly duo.

SUPER-VILLAIN OWNER

BLACK MANTA

ALLIES: **FOES:**

EVIL HENCHFISH

STATS

SECRET BIO:
These finny goodfellas grew up in Atlantis, in the shadow of Storm, Topo, and Tusky, Aquaman's pets. They always felt like second-class sea citizens. So they teamed up with Ocean Master, hoping to overthrow Atlantis and rule by his sea side.

JOHNNY
SPECIES: Swordfish
POWER: Needle nose
FOOD: Vegetable tempura

JOEY
SPECIES: Swordfish
POWER: Sharp snout
FOOD: Cuttlefish

FRANKIE
SPECIES: Anglerfish
POWER: Bright ideas
FOOD: Anglefood cake

GEORGE
SPECIES: Blowfish
POWER: Swollen head
FOOD: Cream puffs

SUPER-VILLAIN OWNER
OCEAN MASTER

ALLIES:  *FOES:*

X-43

SPECIES: Cyborg Newt
BIRTHPLACE: Central City
FOOD: Newtle casserole

Power Saw Arm

Computer Brain

FUN FACT!

X-43 must remember not to twiddle his thumbs or thumb wrestle with himself.

Robot Armor

Whip Tail

BIT BIT

SPECIES: Cyborg Newt
BIRTHPLACE: Central City
FOOD: Chicken newtle soup

LASER EYE
Has 2000/2000 vision.

Power Claw Arm

Robot Armor

What did the salamander say to the toad?

"Warts new?"

STATS

SECRET BIO:
After being rescued from a lowly pet shop, these cyborg newts quickly got up to speed on their owner's evil ways. But keeping up with their master, Reverse Flash, is not easy. These savvy salamanders use brain power to feed their speed and pump up their power. Rapid, raging robots are their preferred mode of travel.

SUPER-VILLAIN OWNER
REVERSE FLASH

ALLIES: FOES:

ADMIRAL PEARY

Blizzard Vision

Leadership

Tracking

THICK COAT
Protects against sub-zero temperatures.

STATS

SPECIES: Husky
BIRTHPLACE: Alaska
FOOD: Cold cuts

SUPER-VILLAIN OWNER
CAPTAIN COLD

ALLIES: FOES:

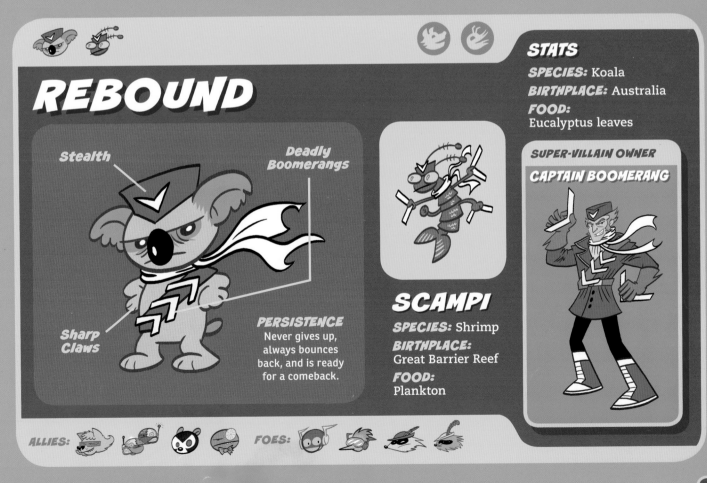

REBOUND

Stealth

Deadly Boomerangs

Sharp Claws

PERSISTENCE
Never gives up, always bounces back, and is ready for a comeback.

SCAMPI

SPECIES: Shrimp
BIRTHPLACE: Great Barrier Reef
FOOD: Plankton

STATS

SPECIES: Koala
BIRTHPLACE: Australia
FOOD: Eucalyptus leaves

SUPER-VILLAIN OWNER
CAPTAIN BOOMERANG

ALLIES: FOES:

SINESTRO BUG CORPS
Yellow Lanterns, Space Sector -0

TOOTZ *(LEADER)*

SPECIES: Stink Bug
POWER: Gas clouds
FOOD: Limburger cheese

EEZIX

SPECIES: Mosquito
POWER: Power drain
FOOD: Plasma

WAXXEE

SPECIES: Earwig
POWER: Mind control
FOOD: Ear wax

DONALD

SPECIES: Cockroach
POWER: Dirty mouth
FOOD: Garbage

FIMBLE

SPECIES: Stick Insect
POWER: Mimicry
FOOD: Lettuce

STATS

SECRET BIO:
The creepy crawly critters of the Sinestro Bug Corps use their yellow rings to spread fear across the universe.

RUINING APPETITES
These indecent insects love nothing more than to be the flies in your soup or the ants at your picnic.

WEBBIK

SPECIES: Tarantula
POWER: Fear webs
FOOD: Newts

FURRY FACTS!

ARACHNOPHOBIA!
Webbik is a master of preying on an enemy's fear of creepy-crawlies. His fear web captures his foes in its nightmarish grasp.

NOT A BUG!
Don't call Webbik an insect—it really bugs him! A tarantula is an arachnid!

A LEG UP!
Like all tarantulas, Webbik can regenerate lost limbs, giving him a leg up on his enemies.

SUPER-VILLAIN PAL

SINESTRO
Yellow Lantern,
Space Sector -0

SINESTRO DOG CORPS
Yellow Lanterns, Space Sector -0

SNORRT
BREED: Pug
POWER: Smell-o-location
FOOD: Stinky cheese

PRONTO
BREED: Jackal
POWER: Teleportation
FOOD: Flapjacks

WHOOSH
BREED: Greyhound
POWER: Windstorms
FOOD: Baked beans

ROLF
BREED: Rottweiler
POWER: Plant life eradication
FOOD: Brats and crullers

STATS

SECRET BIO:
When Sinestro, the renegade Green Lantern, recruited other outlaws to his new Sinestro Corps, he gathered these malevolent mutts from the reaches of deep space. Their power rings will make mincemeat of anyone who gets in their way. Don't mess with these dawgs—you're barking up the wrong tree!

SUPER-VILLAIN PAL

SINESTRO
Yellow Lantern,
Space Sector -0

ALLIES: **FOES:**

KAJUNN
Yellow Lantern, Space Sector -0

Snapping Jaws

Sharp Talons

Agility

Powerful Tail

STATS
SPECIES: Alligator
BIRTHPLACE: New Orleans
FOOD: Yellowfin tuna

SUPER-VILLAIN PAL
ROMAT-RU
Yellow Lantern,
Space Sector -0

ALLIES: **FOES:**

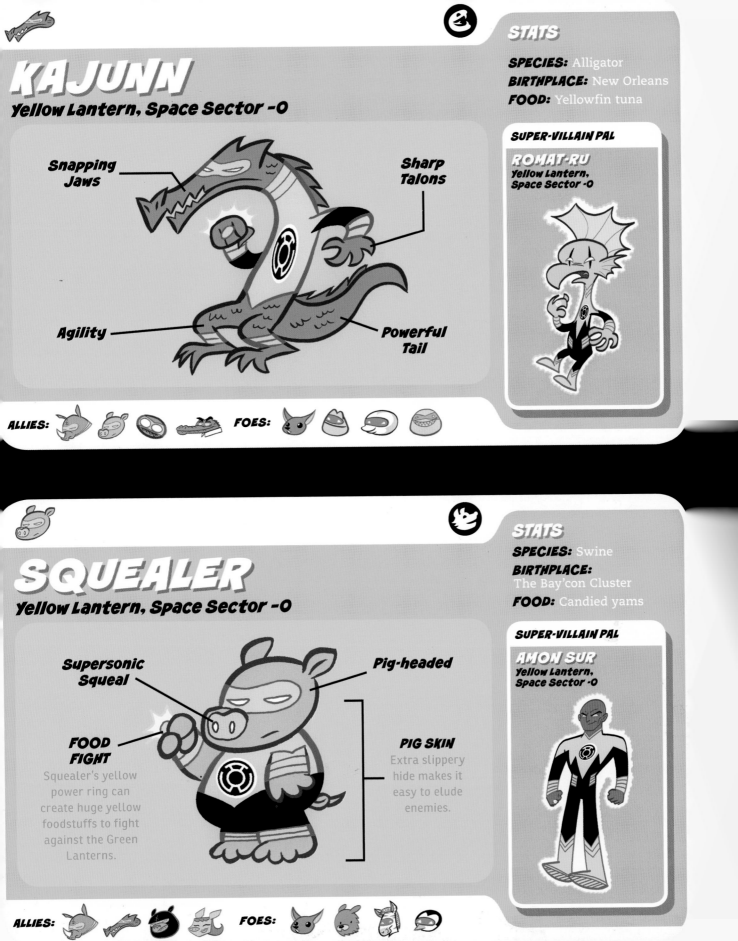

SQUEALER
Yellow Lantern, Space Sector -0

Supersonic Squeal

Pig-headed

FOOD FIGHT
Squealer's yellow power ring can create huge yellow foodstuffs to fight against the Green Lanterns.

PIG SKIN
Extra slippery hide makes it easy to elude enemies.

STATS
SPECIES: Swine
BIRTHPLACE:
The Bay'con Cluster
FOOD: Candied yams

SUPER-VILLAIN PAL
AMON SUR
Yellow Lantern,
Space Sector -0

ALLIES: **FOES:**

RHINOLDO
Yellow Lantern, Space Sector -O

SECRET BIO:
Thick-skinned and thick-headed, Rhinoldo uses brute strength rather than brains to get what he wants. His master, Arkillo, is the drill sergeant for members of the Sinestro Corps. Rhinoldo trains other Lantern companions to battle alongside Arkillo and defeat the Green Lanterns throughout the universe.

SECRET MOTTO:
"Attack first, ask questions later. Then attack some more!"

Stubborn

THICK HIDE
Natural armor protects against enemy attacks!

Power Horn

POWER RING
Can create contructs out of yellow energy using just his mind.

SUPER-VILLAIN PAL

ARKILLO
Yellow Lantern, Space Sector -O

FUN FACTS!

YELLOW LANTERNS
Yellow is the color of fear throughout the universe, and Rhinoldo's fearsome appearance makes many foes turn tail and run for cover.

YELLOW LANTERN OATH:
"In blackest day, in brightest night, beware your fears made into light. Let those who try to stop what's right, burn like my power...
Sinestro's might!"

ALLIES:     **FOES:**

DEX-STARR
Red Lantern, Space Sector 666

STATS
SPECIES: House cat
BIRTHPLACE: Brooklyn, New York
FOOD: Not picky

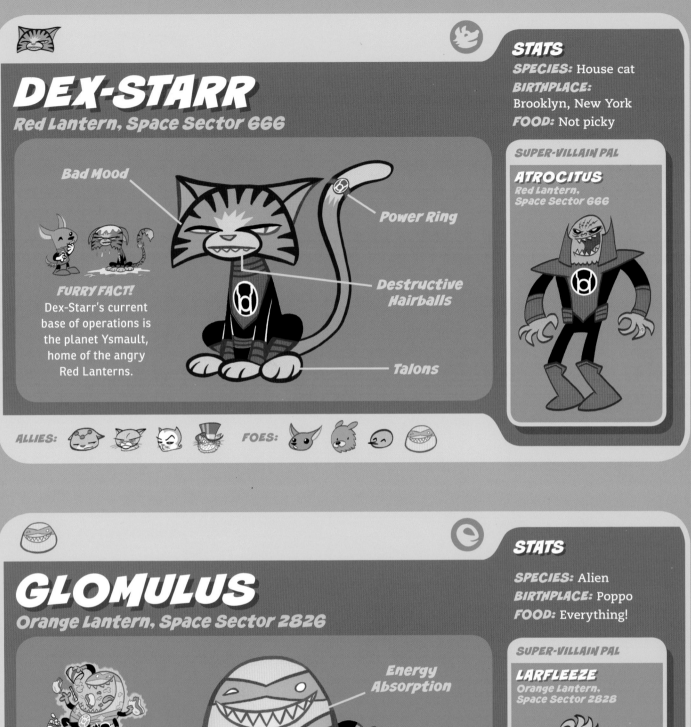

Bad Mood

Power Ring

Destructive Hairballs

Talons

FURRY FACT!
Dex-Starr's current base of operations is the planet Ysmault, home of the angry Red Lanterns.

SUPER-VILLAIN PAL
ATROCITUS
Red Lantern,
Space Sector 666

ALLIES: **FOES:**

GLOMULUS
Orange Lantern, Space Sector 2826

STATS
SPECIES: Alien
BIRTHPLACE: Poppo
FOOD: Everything!

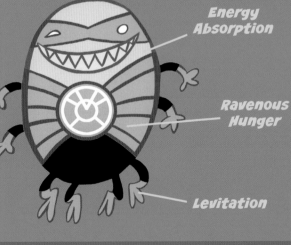

Energy Absorption

Ravenous Hunger

Levitation

NOM-NOM-NOM!
Glomulus is a formidable member of the Orange Lantern Corps, since he can eat anything, including weapons and energy beams.

SUPER-VILLAIN PAL
LARFLEEZE
Orange Lantern,
Space Sector 2828

ALLIES: **FOES:**

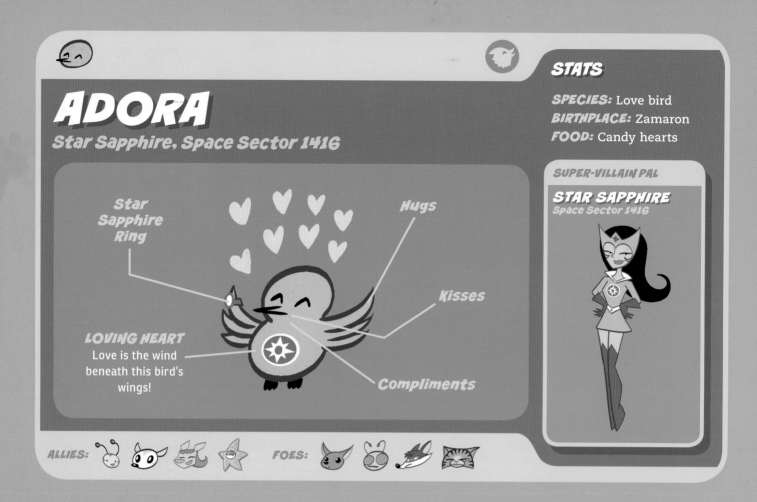

ADORA
Star Sapphire, Space Sector 1416

Star Sapphire Ring

Hugs

Kisses

LOVING HEART
Love is the wind beneath this bird's wings!

Compliments

STATS

SPECIES: Love bird
BIRTHPLACE: Zamaron
FOOD: Candy hearts

SUPER-VILLAIN PAL
STAR SAPPHIRE
Space Sector 1416

ALLIES: **FOES:**

STARROS

Freaky Eyes

Cloning Powers

MIND CONTROL
To move and survive, Starros suction onto the faces of people and pets. While attached, they can make their victims do anything—even play music!

STATS

SPECIES:
Star Conquerors
BIRTHPLACE: Space
FOOD: Space dust

SUPER-VILLAIN OWNER
STARRO

ALLIES: **FOES:**

CAT CRIME CLUB

PURRING PETE

BREED: Space-faring Cat
POWER: *Purr*-fect plans
FOOD: Warm milk

SCRATCHY TOM

BREED: Space-faring Cat
POWER: Prowling
FOOD: Fleas

GAT CAT

BREED: Space-faring Cat
POWER: Hair brawling
FOOD: Minnows

KID KITTY

BREED: Space-faring Cat
POWER: Cat burglary
FOOD: Sardines

STATS

SECRET BIO:
This group of criminal kitties dogs the footsteps of the Space Canine Patrol Agents (*see page* 12). When they're not cat-nabbing loot, they're trying to scratch out the S.C.P.A. The hero dogs will do anything to stop them— or at least put their criminal activities on *paws*.

CRIME SHIP
The C.C.C. travel through space in a cat-shaped ship.

SUPER-VILLAIN PAL

MALLEABLE MAN

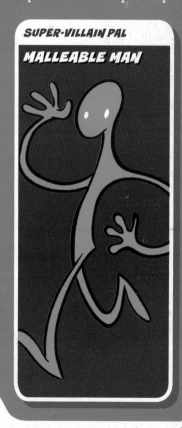

ALLIES: **FOES:**

MR. MIND

SPECIES: Space worm
BIRTHPLACE: Venus
FOOD: Brainwaves

SECRET BIO:
Dangerous things come in small packages—behold, the 2-inch Mr. Mind, a telepathic worm from the planet Venus and leader of the Monster Society of Evil. His mitey mind is mighty, indeed. And though his foes may tend to overlook him, or not even see him, they will obey the hypnotic commands from this puny but powerful parasite.

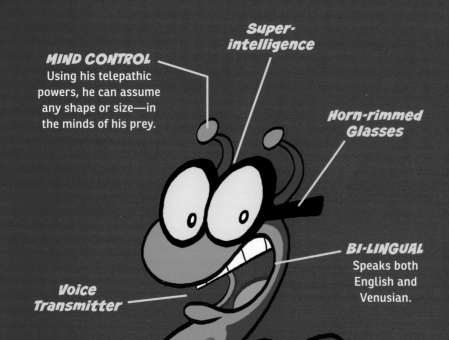

Super-intelligence

MIND CONTROL
Using his telepathic powers, he can assume any shape or size—in the minds of his prey.

Horn-rimmed Glasses

Voice Transmitter

BI-LINGUAL
Speaks both English and Venusian.

FUN FACT!

The last of his species from Venus, Mr. Mind is determined to be the latest and greatest—ruler of all Earth!

What is the best advice to give a worm?
Sleep late!

HOPPED UP
Mr. Mind once trapped Hoppy in a trippy trance, but his plan was soon shattered by the shout of "Shazam!".

SUPER-VILLAIN PARTNER

DR. SIVANA

ALLIES: **FOES:**

SOBEK

STATS

SPECIES: Crocodile
BIRTHPLACE:
Nile River, Egypt
FOOD:
Chocolate bunnies

MEAGER MIND
Although Sobek is big and powerful, his brain is only the size of a pea—like every other crocodile's. No wonder he falls so easily under the mental mastery of Mr. Mind.

JAWS OF STEEL
A crocodile's jaws can chomp with more "bite force" than any other animal on the planet!

Razor-sharp Teeth

Ultra-strength

Knife-like Claws

Powerhouse Tail

SECRET BIO:
As a young crocodile, Sobek was recruited by Mr. Mind to join his Monster Society of Evil. He was named after the Egyptian crocodile god of the Nile River. Since there are no rivers in his current home of Fawcett City, Sobek is content to swim the sewers. Mistake his snappy suit and extra-wide grin for kindness, and you'll be "after while, crocodile" for good.

SUPER-VILLAIN OWNER

BLACK ADAM

REVERSE SHAZAM!
Shazam!'s opposite was created by Wizzo the Wizard from the real Shazam!'s mirror reflection. Mr. Mind hopes to lure him into his bad-guy brigade.

ALLIES: **FOES:**

UNDEAD PET CLUB

SECRET BIO:
You can't keep a good pet down...even if it's buried! These roadkill rascals never say die when they leave their crowded pet cemetery and start stealing swampland. The authorities want to catch this zombie zoo dead or alive—well, mostly dead.

MAMA RIPPLES

BREED: Manx cat
POWER: Howlin'
FOOD: Grisly gumbo

LIMPY

BREED: Possum
POWER: Hangin'
FOOD: Stinky shrimp

FAYE PRECIOUS

BREED: Persian cat
POWER: Hoardin'
FOOD: Crusty cornbread

OFFIE LEE

BREED: Hound Dog
POWER: Houndin'
FOOD: Ooky okra

SUPER-VILLAIN OWNER
SOLOMON GRUNDY

ALLIES: **FOES:**

PATCHES

Horns

THE MIGHTY FALL
The smallest of heroes,
Spot (*see page* 52), found
Patches' weakness.
Sensitive ears!

Roughneck

Giant
Size

Bling

SPECIES: Giraffe
BIRTHPLACE: Africa
FOOD:
Footlong tofu dogs

SECRET BIO:
Patches first grew to
skyscraper size when
the angry Giganta stole
magic powder from
Apache Chief, sprinkled
it on them both, and
chanted the ancient
words: "Inuk-chuk!"

SUPER-VILLAIN OWNER

GIGANTA

ALLIES: FOES:

RAZOR

SPECIES: White tiger
BIRTHPLACE: Gotham City Zoo
FOOD: Marshmallows

SECRET BIO:
Deathstroke may be a master assassin, but even cold-hearted criminals need friends. So, Deathstroke re-created the experiment that gave him his enhanced intellect and powers for Razor. While it's not true that cats have nine lives—this one has nine times the intellect, stamina, strength, and speed of your average kitty cat!

Enhanced Intellect

Feline Instincts

NTH METAL ARMOR
Like his owner, Razor wears Nth Metal armor that is even stronger than titanium!

"Razor"-sharp Claws

Enhanced Body

FURRY FACT!

KUNG FU–TIGER STYLE!
This aggressive form of kung fu features an open fist, making Razor's claws even more dangerous!

Unlike Deathstroke, Razor still has both of his eyes—but he often keeps one eye closed during combat in honor of his owner.

SUPER-VILLAIN OWNER

DEATHSTROKE

ALLIES: **FOES:**

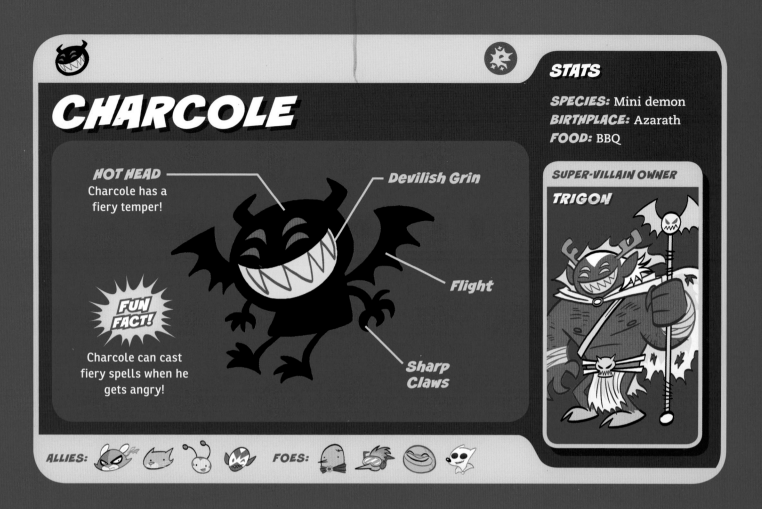

CHARCOLE

STATS

SPECIES: Mini demon
BIRTHPLACE: Azarath
FOOD: BBQ

HOT HEAD
Charcole has a fiery temper!

Devilish Grin

Flight

Sharp Claws

FUN FACT!

Charcole can cast fiery spells when he gets angry!

SUPER-VILLAIN OWNER

TRIGON

ALLIES: **FOES:**

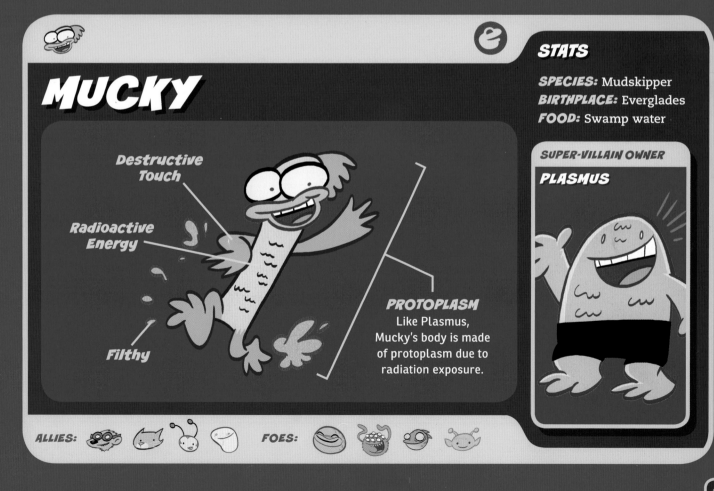

MUCKY

STATS

SPECIES: Mudskipper
BIRTHPLACE: Everglades
FOOD: Swamp water

Destructive Touch

Radioactive Energy

Filthy

PROTOPLASM
Like Plasmus, Mucky's body is made of protoplasm due to radiation exposure.

SUPER-VILLAIN OWNER

PLASMUS

ALLIES: **FOES:**

THE FURSOME FIVE

PSYCHE

SPECIES: Butterfly
POWER: Telepathy
FOOD: Insects

KIKI

SPECIES: Cat
POWER: Black magic
FOOD: Salt herring

SHEILA

SPECIES: Flying squirrel
POWER: Furious flight
FOOD: Nectar

SUPER-VILLAIN OWNER

PSIMON

SUPER-VILLAIN OWNER

JINX

SUPER-VILLAIN OWNER

SHIMMER

THE FEARSOME FIVE

GADGET

SPECIES: Meerkat
POWER: Cool devices
FOOD: Centipedes

IVAN

SPECIES: Wooly mammoth
POWER: Sniffing snout
FOOD: Veggies

SUPER-VILLAIN OWNER
GIZMO

SUPER-VILLAIN OWNER
MAMMOTH

STATS

SECRET BIO:
The evil Dr. Light created the Fearsome Five to defeat the heroic Teen Titans. However, this posse of problem children soon grew lonely in their no-good lifestyles. So they each adopted a powerful Villain Pet! Soon, this quintuplet of pets formed their own evil organization, known as the Fursome Five.

FUN FACT!

Led by the bitty butterfly Psyche, the Fursome Five will stop at nothing to defeat the pets of the Teen Titans.

VILLAIN PETS SIZE CHART!

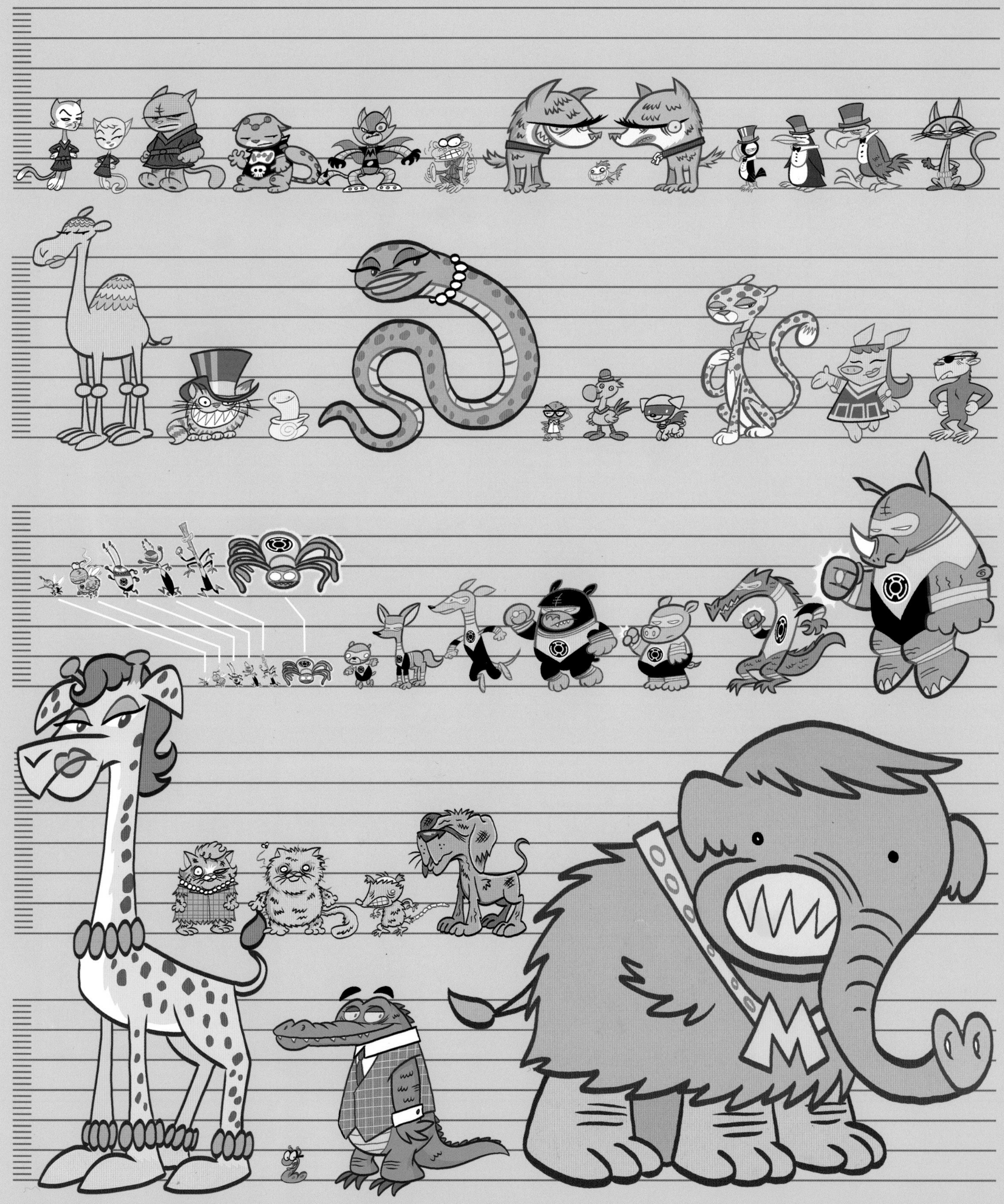

PETS WITH POWER!

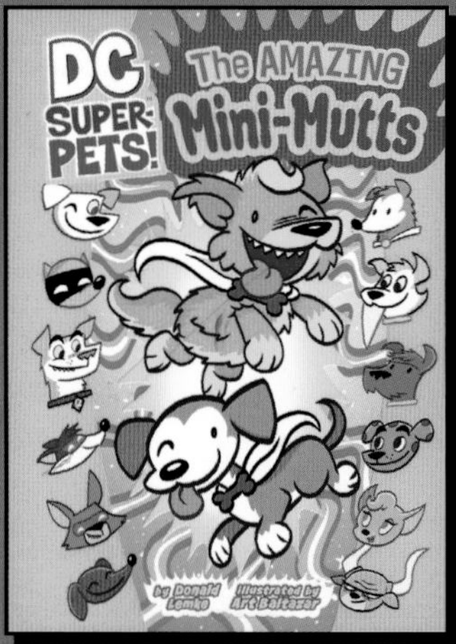
DC SUPER-PETS!
The AMAZING Mini-Mutts
by Donald Lemke
illustrated by Art Baltazar

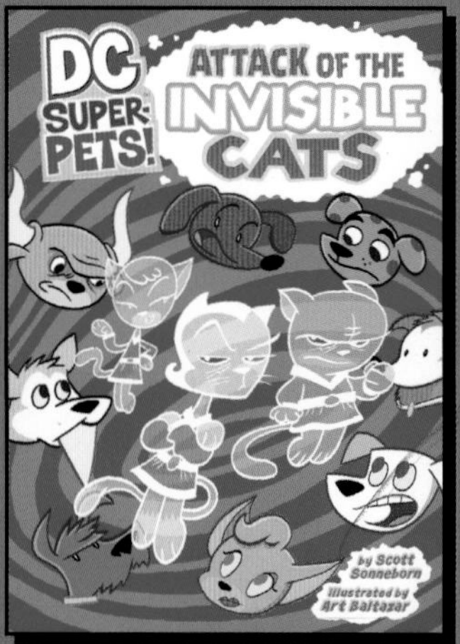
DC SUPER-PETS!
ATTACK OF THE INVISIBLE CATS
by Scott Sonneborn
illustrated by Art Baltazar

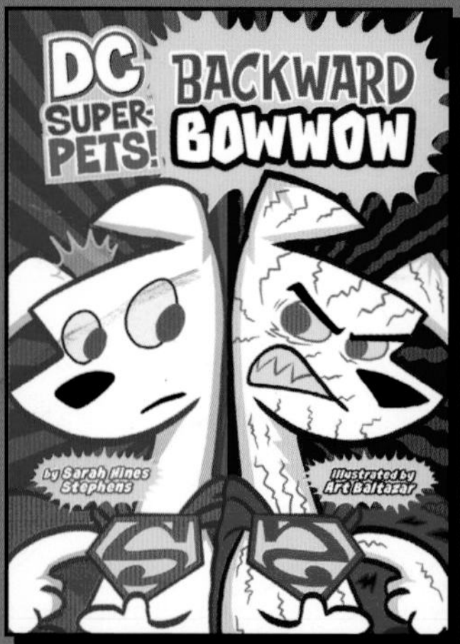
DC SUPER-PETS!
BACKWARD BOWWOW
by Sarah Hines Stephens
illustrated by Art Baltazar

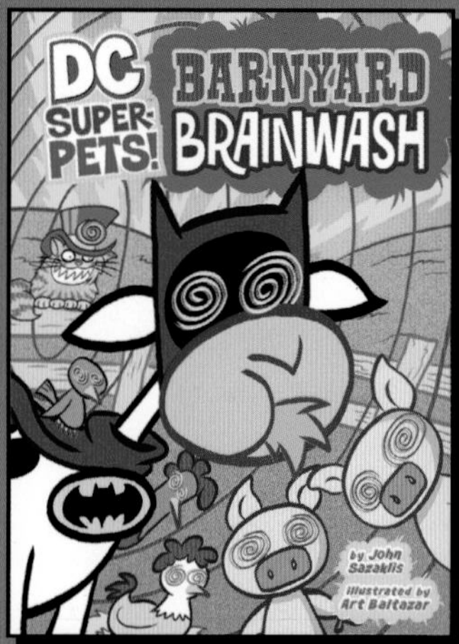
DC SUPER-PETS!
BARNYARD BRAINWASH
by John Sazaklis
illustrated by Art Baltazar

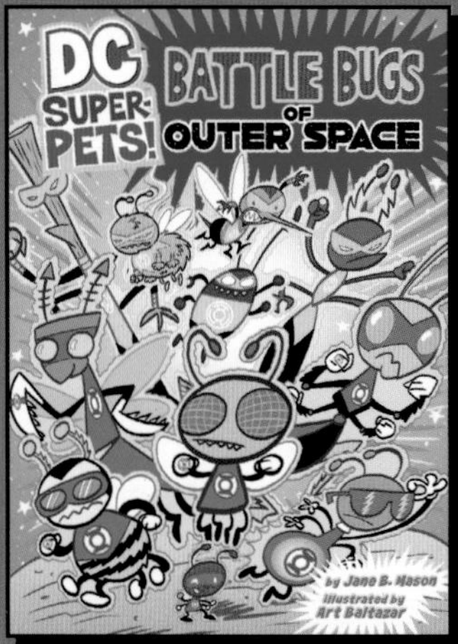
DC SUPER-PETS!
BATTLE BUGS OF OUTER SPACE
by Jane B. Mason
illustrated by Art Baltazar

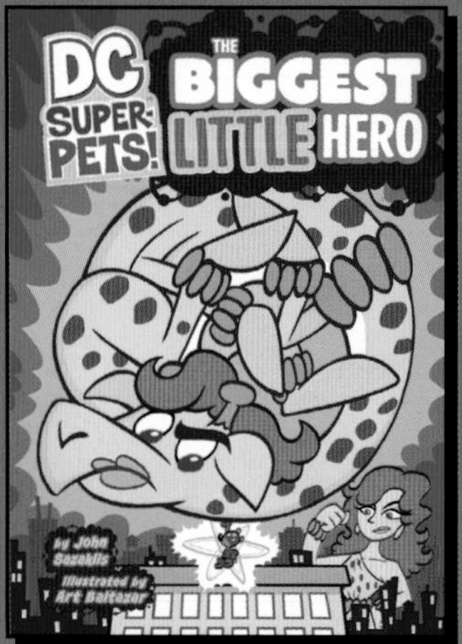
DC SUPER-PETS!
THE BIGGEST LITTLE HERO
by John Sazaklis
illustrated by Art Baltazar

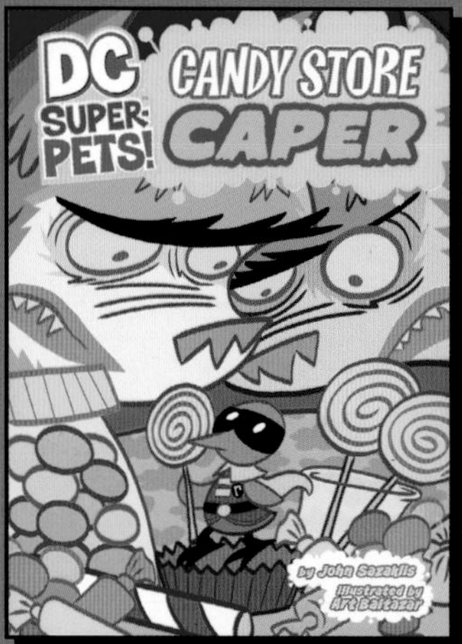
DC SUPER-PETS!
CANDY STORE CAPER
by John Sazaklis
illustrated by Art Baltazar

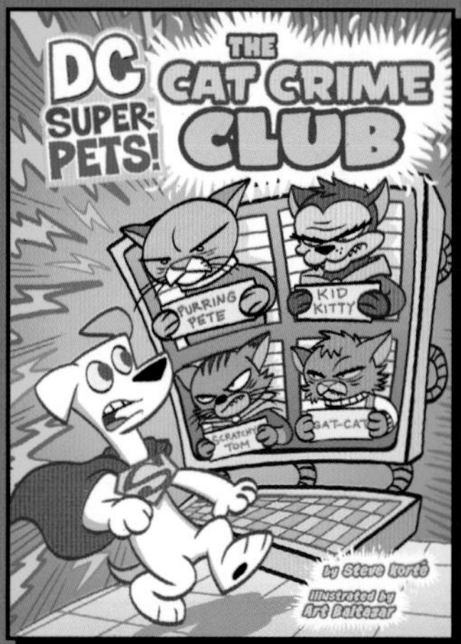
DC SUPER-PETS!
THE CAT CRIME CLUB
PURRING PETE
KID KITTY
SCRATCHY TOM
BAT-CAT
by Steve Korté
illustrated by Art Baltazar

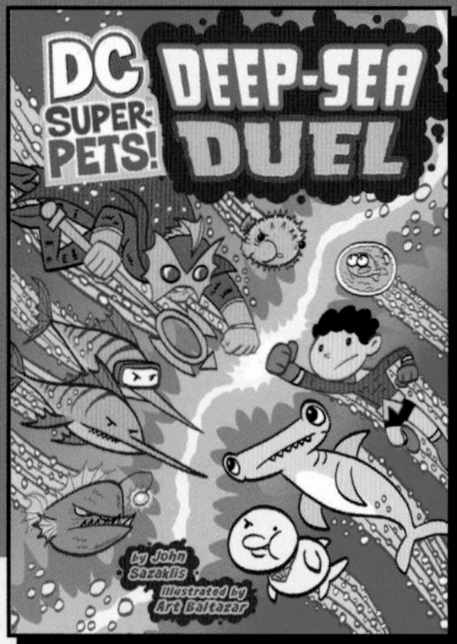
DC SUPER-PETS!
DEEP-SEA DUEL
by John Sazaklis
illustrated by Art Baltazar

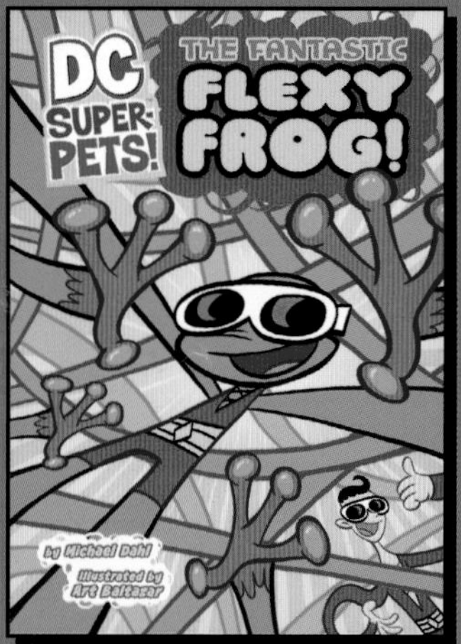
DC SUPER-PETS!
THE FANTASTIC FLEXY FROG!
by Michael Dahl
illustrated by Art Baltazar

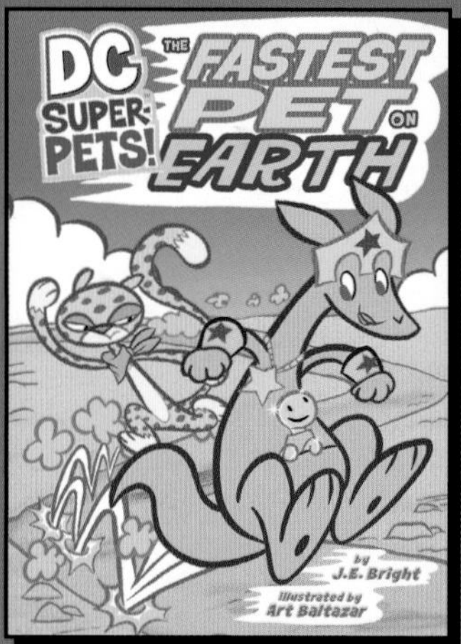
DC SUPER-PETS!
THE FASTEST PET ON EARTH
by J.E. Bright
illustrated by Art Baltazar

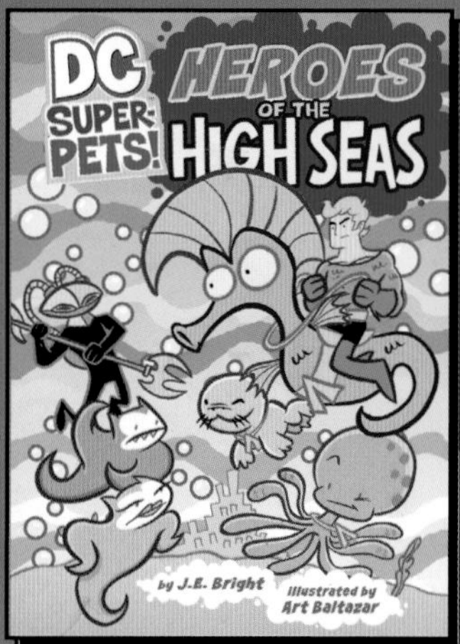
DC SUPER-PETS!
HEROES OF THE HIGH SEAS
by J.E. Bright
illustrated by Art Baltazar

Read all of these totally awesome chapter books, starring your favorite DC SUPER-PETS!

INDEX!

CREDITS AND MORE!

CAPSTONE

Editor & Contributing Writer
Donald Lemke

Art Director & Designer
Bob Lentz

Publisher Ashley C. Andersen Zantop
Editorial Director Michael Dahl
Assistant Editor Sean Tulien
Creative Director Heather Kindseth
Production Specialist Kathy McColley

The Capstone Team would like to thank the following:

Art Baltazar; Benjamin Harper, Geoff Johns, and everyone at Warner Bros.
Consumer Products and DC Entertainment; John Sazaklis, Sarah Hines
Stephens, J.E. Bright, Jane Mason, Scott Sonneborn, and Steve Korté.

ACKNOWLEDGEMENTS

Superman created by Jerry Siegel and Joe Shuster.
Supergirl based on characters created by Jerry Siegel and Joe Shuster.
By special arrangement with the Jerry Siegel family.
Batman created by Bob Kane.
Wonder Woman created by William Moulton Marston.
Aquaman created by Paul Norris.
Hawkman and The Atom/Ray Palmer created by Gardner Fox.
Plastic Man created by Jack Cole.
Swamp Thing created by Len Wein and Bernie Wrightson.
Lobo created by Roger Slifer and Keith Giffen.

Artist credits: Alex Toth, Art Baltazar, Curt Swan, George Klein,
Harry G. Peter, Jimmy Thompson, Martin Naydel, Nick Cardy,
Sheldon Moldoff, and Stan Kaye.

MEET THE AUTHOR!

Steve Korté

Steve Korté is a DC Comics archivist and the editor of *75 Years of DC Comics*, winner of the 2011 Eisner Award, and *Jack Cole and Plastic Man*, winner of the 2002 Harvey Award. He lives in New York City with his own super-cat, Duke.

MEET THE ILLUSTRATOR!

Eisner Award-winner *Art Baltazar*

Art Baltazar is a cartoonist machine from the heart of Chicago! He defines cartoons and comics not only as an art style, but as a way of life. Currently, Art is the creative force behind *The New York Times* best-selling, Eisner Award-winning, DC Comics series *Tiny Titans*, and the co-writer for *Billy Batson and the Magic of SHAZAM!* Art is living the dream! He draws comics and never has to leave the house. He lives with his lovely wife, Rose, big boy Sonny, little boy Gordon, and little girl Audrey. Right on!

Picture Window Books

A Capstone Imprint
1710 Roe Crest Drive
North Mankato, MN 56003
www.capstonepub.com

Published in 2013

Cataloging-in-Publication Data is available at the Library of Congress website.
ISBN: 978-1-4795-2030-5 (library binding)
ISBN: 978-1-4048-8297-3 (trade paperback)

Printed in China.
009952R

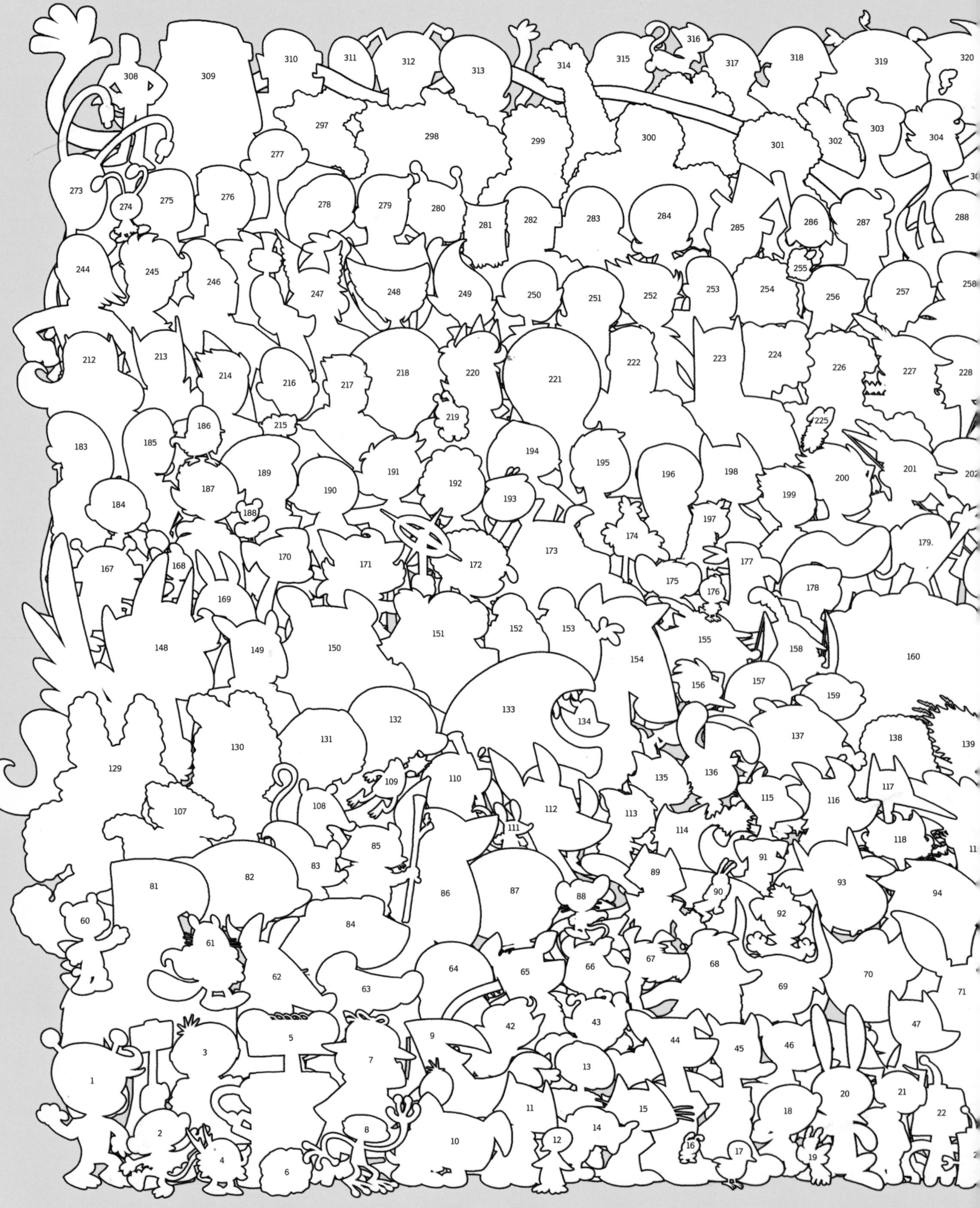

1. Zook
2. Haley
3. Steel Turtle
4. Scarabian Knight
5. Computo
6. Thud
7. Detective Chimp
8. Plastic Frog
9. Big Ted
10. Dawg
11. Whizzy
12. Zallion
13. Super-Turtle
14. Hot Dog
15. Streaky
16. Eeny
17. Robin Robin
18. Beppo
19. Zhoomp
20. Hoppy
21. Whatzit
22. F.E.L.I.X.
23. M.A.X.
24. Banjo
25. X-43
26. Bit Bit
27. Fimble
28. Ignatius
29. Webbik
30. Rozz
31. Donald
32. Omegan
33. Waxxee
34. Dex-Starr
35. Mr. Mind
36. Dogwood
37. Mad Catter
38. Dr. Spider
39. Lefty
40. Goop
41. Osito
42. Gleek
43. Proty
44. Krypto
45. Ace
46. Paw Pooch
47. Shadow
48. Giggles
49. Crackers
50. Mechanikat
51. Brainicat
52. Bizarro Krypto
53. Fer-El
54. General Manx
55. Nizz
56. Anna Conda
57. Squealer
58. Dribodod
59. Destructo
60. Spot
61. Super-Squirrel
62. Gumshoe
63. Geoffrey
64. Ark
65. Rex the Wonder Dog
66. Tusky Husky
67. Tail Terrier
68. Chameleon Collie
69. Bull Dog
70. Mammoth Mutt
71. Captain Carrot
72. Ace-Mite
73. Joker Fish
74. Sneezers
75. Misty
76. Sobek
77. Purring Pete
78. Kid Kitty
79. Gat Cat
80. Scratchy Tom
81. Chuk
82. Zilwondra
83. Mossy
84. Loafers
85. Starlene
86. Stripezoid
87. Topo
88. Fuzzy
89. Atomic Tom
90. Gratch
91. Freckles
92. Prophetic Pup
93. Batcow
94. Tawky Tawny
95. Gryll
96. Griff
97. Artie Puffin
98. Waddles
99. Faye Precious
100. Mama Ripples
101. Chauncey
102. Limpy
103. Croward
104. Frankie
105. Joey
106. George
107. Sen-Tag
108. Merle
109. Ribitz
110. Salty the Aquadog
111. Leepa
112. Jumpa
113. Crab Tabby
114. Power Puss
115. Scoop
116. Gutenberg
117. Blue
118. Misty
119. Tarvos
120. Ice Bear
121. Admiral Peary
122. Rebound
123. Glomulus
124. Otto
125. Offie Lee
126. Johnny
127. Sāndy
128. Rhinoldo
129. Fendor
130. G'nort
131. Tusky
132. Porpy
133. Storm
134. Jimmy the Mussel
135. Stinky
136. Tibbar
137. Dusty
138. Zinkk
139. Sparklzz
140. Como
141. Scampi
142. Kiki
143. Snorrt
144. Pronto
145. Whoosh
146. Rolf
147. Kajunn
148. Jewellion
149. Dr. Canus
150. Prince Tuftan
151. King
152. Stranger
153. Strangest
154. Comet
155. Quiver
156. Lightning Rodney
157. Silky
158. Quill
159. Guacamole
160. K'uddles
161. Titano
162. Razor
163. Gadget
164. Ivan
165. Patches
166. Sheila
167. Intello
168. Anti-Matt